OZARK OMENS

OZARK OMENS

HEDGE WITCH DIARIES™ BOOK 3

THEOPHILUS MONROE

MICHAEL ANDERLE

LMBPN® Publishing
2375 E. Tropicana Avenue, Suite 8-305
Las Vegas, Nevada 89119 USA

Version 1.00, December 2023
ebook ISBN: 979-8-88878-370-2
Print ISBN: 979-8-88878-726-7

THE OZARK OMENS TEAM

Thanks to our JIT Readers
Christopher Gilliard
Dorothy Lloyd
Jan Hunnicutt
Dave Hicks

If We've missed anyone, please let us know!

Editor
The SkyFyre Editing Team

CHAPTER ONE

The dead were walking among us, and it was all my fault.

I've always been able to see spirits. Dead animals, mostly. These days, no one needed a sixth sense to see dead folk. They were rising faster than a teenage boy with a Victoria's Secret catalog. And no one wanted to see a stiff—or a stiffy—popping up where it didn't belong.

So far, the resurrections were limited to the region around the lake. If what we read in the Book of the Dead was true, it was only a matter of time before the problem spread.

These dead weren't zombies. No snarling, grunting, or taste for brains. They appeared the same as they were in life. They went back to their families.

But the prophecy in the book said the dead would rise to rule the world.

Maybe the dead were ignorant of their destiny. Maybe they were biding their time until they had the numbers to make a serious play at world domination. So far, no one had risen who hadn't died *recently*. It wasn't like ancient badasses from the past were coming back to lead armies or whatever. Rednecks, fishermen, and drowned drunk boaters. Not the kind of folk anyone would ever mistake for a threat to the world order.

I suspected even that was bound to change sooner or later.

When I wasn't working, Gareth and I were hitting the local cemeteries and checking for disturbed graves. If we caught anyone trying to claw their way out of the ground, I could put on my Isis ring, access my goddess powers, and stop it.

Not like it would do much good. With the veil between the living and the dead thinner than plastic wrap, dropping the dead was like a game of whack-a-mole. The playing board was too big, even if the resurrections were local, and I was the only mallet capable of bopping the dead on the head.

At least I was the only one who could stop them from rising before it was too late. Before they came to, remembered who they were, and returned to their families. Sure, someone could knock them off later in the usual way. At that point, it got all sticky. Ethically and legally speaking.

As I trudged through the cemetery with Gareth, I couldn't help but feel like we were playing a losing game. The dead kept popping up with no way to predict where they would come from next. It was like trying to plug a leaky dam with a sieve.

"Briar, you okay?" Gareth asked with concern etched on his face.

I nodded, trying to shake off the feeling of dread settling over me. "Yeah, I'm good. Just tired, I guess."

He didn't look convinced, but he didn't press the issue. "Are you mad at me?"

I sighed. Freaking men and their insecurities. Couldn't a girl have a little PMS without the men in their lives thinking we were angry at them? "Why would you think I'm mad at you?"

Gareth shrugged. "I don't know. I was the one who asked you to raise the people I'd killed. I was wrong…"

I took a deep breath. "Yeah, you were, but it's not like you knew better. You were trying to fix your past. If I could fix the past, I'd do a few things differently, too."

"Like Dorian?" Gareth asked.

There went the insecurities again. This time, they were legit. Gareth wasn't my boyfriend. Not exactly. I suspected he thought of himself that way. I hadn't bothered to correct him, and in my vulnerability after Dorian left, he became my rebound.

Usually, when you rebound, you have your fun, then move on. With Gareth, I needed him. He was the most powerful witch around. I also didn't know if or when Dorian would ever come back. He'd told me to move on with my life. Do what I needed to do. He didn't say to do *who* I needed to, but I wasn't coloring outside the lines. When a dude leaves, says he loves you, but tells you to move on, how are you supposed to take it?

Dorian went to Egypt. He was trying to unravel this whole Isis mystery. If I were the reincarnation of a goddess, was there a way to embrace my ancient power without reviving my ancient personality? I didn't want to lose who I was in a sea of divine memories. This life was what mattered.

The idea of who I was being swallowed up by who I might have been in the past was a little like death. I wasn't sure if I let myself *become* Isis, I'd ever be able to raise Briar Bloom from the grave of my mind again.

"Over there." I pointed to a mound of dirt that looked recently disturbed.

Gareth knelt and began digging with a small spade he'd brought with him. "I think you're right. The dirt is loose, going down pretty deep."

I gulped. "Look at the marker."

Gareth sighed. "He was only a kid. Twelve years old when he died."

I huffed. "I'm not sure I'd have the heart to stop him if we'd caught him in time. Still, if he rose, what are the chances a twelve-year-old knows his way home?"

"There's no telling how long it's been since he rose. At the least, we need to find his family. They need to know their boy…" I leaned in and examined the gravestone more closely. "… that Andrew is back."

Gareth shook his head. "Can you imagine?"

I shrugged. "Imagine what?"

"Losing a child is probably the hardest thing a parent could ever go through. To hear your son is *back* from the dead? I mean, these dead people have done no one any harm. There's no reason to believe they're forming some kind of army to dominate the world…"

I folded my arms. "Except for the fact that Anubis showed up at my trailer and told us this was the end of the world."

Gareth scratched his head. "There's that. Maybe he was wrong? He didn't tell us much. Balzac was supposedly a reincarnated god as well. He got a few things wrong."

"Well, it would be convenient for you if Anubis was full of crap. Then you wouldn't have to feel so guilty about asking me to clean up your mistakes."

Gareth stared at me blankly. "I was asking you to bring people back who I murdered while I was consumed with dark magic, Briar. We're talking about murder, not a mistake. Besides, in case you forget, I only embraced dark magic to save you from the Réminians."

I sighed. "I remember. Look, there's no reason to point fingers. Casting blame is like casting a rod with nothing but a hook and a bobber into the lake. It's a waste of time, and you'll never reel anything in."

Gareth rubbed his brow. "You're right. I'm sorry. This whole situation has me distressed."

"You and me both," I admitted. "This is the first kid we've found raised, though. I'm worried about him. We need to find him."

Gareth nodded. "You're right. We could look up his family

and see if Andrew found his way home. But his last name is Williams. I'm betting there are a few dozen Williams with residences around the lake."

I nodded. "We have a date of birth and death. We can look up his obit. That should give us more information on his family and their whereabouts."

Gareth tilted his head. "What if there's a faster way?"

I bit my lip. "What are you thinking?"

"Use your abilities! Not your Isis abilities. Your Briar abilities. If an undead kid rose here, certainly there's an animal spirit or two nearby that saw something."

I nodded thoughtfully. "It's worth a shot."

I took a deep breath and closed my eyes, focusing on the animal spirits around us. They were there, always watching, always observing. I only needed to find one who had seen something.

Suddenly, I felt a presence nearby. It was a fox spirit, her ghostly form lurking near the tree line surrounding the cemetery. I stepped toward her cautiously. Most animal spirits were drawn to me, but sometimes, they could be skittish the first time we met. I didn't blame them. Most animals ran from humans. I was the first one who'd seen the fox since she died, which could have been yesterday or centuries ago. There was no way to know.

I knelt in front of the spirit fox. She inclined her head and met my gaze.

"Hello, little one. Did you see a young boy rise from the grave? We're looking for him."

The fox tilted her head. My spirit familiars weren't cartoons. They couldn't speak, but I had a connection to the creatures. Somehow, I understood what they meant to tell me. Sort of a gut feeling.

"I think she knows something," I told Gareth before turning back to the fox. "Can you show us where he went?"

The fox spirit nodded and led us through the woods. I

followed closely behind, Gareth at my side. We trudged through the thick brush, keeping our eyes peeled for any sign of movement. The fox seemed to know where she was going and didn't hesitate as she led us deeper into the woods.

After several minutes of travel, we came upon a small clearing. In the center of the clearing was a small, run-down cabin. Smoke billowed from the chimney.

"Is this it?" I asked the fox, who nodded in response.

Gareth and I approached the cabin cautiously, unsure of what we would find inside. We knocked on the door, and after a few moments, it creaked open to reveal an elderly woman. Of course it was an old woman. I suspected she was preparing an Andrew stew at that very moment.

"Can I help you?" she asked, peering at us through thick-rimmed glasses.

"We're looking for a boy named Andrew Williams. We believe he passed through the woods here alone," I explained, watching the woman's face closely for any sign of recognition.

Her expression remained neutral, but I sensed a flicker of fear in her eyes.

"I don't know what you're talking about." Her voice trembled slightly.

"We're not here to hurt anyone," Gareth chimed in. "We only want to make sure Andrew is safe."

The woman hesitated before finally stepping aside and allowing us to enter. The inside of the cabin was dimly lit, and the air was thick with the scent of burning wood.

"Andrew?" I called softly, scanning the room for any sign of the boy.

I noticed movement in the corner and saw a small figure huddled on the floor, hiding behind a pile of blankets.

"It's okay, Andrew. We're not going to hurt you," I reassured him, approaching slowly. "We want to make sure you're safe and that your family knows you're back."

The boy peeked out from behind the blankets, his eyes wide with fear. "I-I don't understand. What's happening?"

Gareth knelt beside me. "Andrew, you died. You were buried in the cemetery nearby, but you came back. Do you remember anything?"

Andrew shook his head, tears welling up in his eyes. "N-no, I don't remember anything. I woke up, and I was so scared. I didn't know where to go but ended up here."

I felt a pang of sympathy for the young boy. To come back from the dead and not remember anything would be terrifying. "We're going to help you, Andrew. We'll find your family and make sure they know you're back. First, we need to make sure you're safe. Can you come with us?"

Andrew hesitated, his wide eyes meeting the old woman's. Something strange was going on here. Who was this woman?

Before we could ask any more questions, the old woman spoke up. "You can't take him. He's my grandson now. I won't let you separate us."

Gareth and I exchanged a look. This was not what we were expecting.

"Your grandson?" I asked, trying to keep my tone neutral. "What do you mean?"

The woman's lips twisted into a snarl. "I mean exactly what I said. He's mine now, and I won't let you take him from me."

I felt a chill run down my spine. Something was definitely off about this situation. "Andrew, do you know this woman? Is she your grandmother?"

The boy shook his head, still looking frightened and confused. "I don't know her."

Gareth and I shared a look. This woman was clearly lying, and the fact that she had taken in a boy who had risen from the dead was suspicious.

"Ma'am, we want to make sure Andrew is safe," Gareth stated, keeping his tone calm. "If you could let us take him to the authorities, they can help us figure out what happened to him and get him back to his family."

The woman's face twisted into a sneer. "I don't trust the authorities. They wouldn't understand what's happened here. They'd take him away from me."

I took a step forward. "Ma'am, we're not leaving without Andrew. He deserves to be with his family and get the help he needs."

The woman's eyes narrowed, and I felt the tension rising. Suddenly, she lunged forward, grabbing a nearby fireplace poker and swinging it at Gareth. He ducked in time, but we both knew this situation was escalating quickly.

"Andrew, come with us!" I shouted, grabbing the boy's hand and pulling him toward the door.

The woman waved her hand, and the cabin door slammed shut. A shimmering magical barrier appeared, sealing the door and blocking our exit.

"You're a witch?" Gareth gasped. "I was the leader of the Morai. How don't I know you?"

The woman cackled. "A witch? Please, dear. I'm a goddess! I'm here to ensure this boy fulfills his purpose."

Gareth grabbed my arm. I still held Andrew tight. Gareth traced his finger through the air to cast a portal spell. Before he could finish, the woman waved her hand again, and a powerful gust of wind blew his magic away.

"What do you mean you're a goddess?" I asked.

The woman approached me, her eyes wide and blazing with a magic I didn't recognize. "Come now, sweet Isis. Don't tell me you don't remember me."

I grunted. "My name is Briar."

"You are Isis! You cannot deny your destiny."

"Destiny can kiss my ass!" I shouted.

The woman scowled. "The boy must be protected."

"Um, yeah. That's what I'm doing."

"You don't *know* what you're doing. You don't even understand who you are!"

A loud *crack* sounded from outside the cabin. The floorboards shook under my feet. "What the…"

The woman sneered at me. "This is your fault!"

"*What* is my fault?" I asked, steadying myself. Before the woman could answer, the entire cabin burst into a million splinters. Only the floor remained.

Anubis appeared as he had before. The woman took two steps back, trembling. Anubis raised his hand to the woman's throat, turned his jackal head toward me, and nodded.

"That's our cue!" I grabbed Gareth while I held onto Andrew with my other hand. Quickly, Gareth formed a portal, and it sucked us in.

We arrived safely back at my trailer. "Are you all right?" I asked the boy.

Andrew nodded, his lips quivering. "I think so. Can I go home now?"

"I think we can arrange that. Do you know your address?"

"I do. Thank you, ma'am. I'm not sure what's going on, but…"

"Don't worry about it." Gareth ruffled the boy's hair. This kid wasn't a threat. He couldn't be. What that woman who called herself a goddess wanted with him remained a mystery. Anubis showing up to aid our escape only added to the enigma.

For now, this poor kid who'd died before his time had another chance to live. All this resurrection business might portend the end of the world, according to the lore of an ancient Egyptian book. But if we could bring this boy home, perhaps a little good, a little peace, could arrive amid the chaos. At least for his family.

CHAPTER TWO

The screen door slammed behind us as we stepped onto the creaky wooden porch. My heart pounded against my ribs like a caged bird. There was no way to know how people would respond when their deceased loved one returned. Some were overcome with joy. Others were terrified. With news of resurrections in the area becoming commonplace, I hoped the reunion wouldn't be as jarring as the first few Gareth and I witnessed after we resurrected the people Gareth killed.

Mrs. Williams flung open the front door, her face slack with shock. For a long moment, she stared, eyes round as quarters, before letting loose a wail that could wake the dead. Which I guess was appropriate, given the situation.

"Andrew!" She threw her arms around the kid, squeezing him tight. Andrew squirmed in her embrace, clearly uncomfortable with the sudden display of emotion. But hey, we could cut the woman some slack. She thought her son was gone forever.

"Oh, sweet boy," she sobbed into his hair. "My sweet, sweet boy. You've come home."

Andrew's dad barreled into the room with his worn flannel

shirt half-tucked into his jeans. "What in tarnation is going on here?" He froze when he saw us standing on the porch.

"Dad," Andrew called softly.

That single word unleashed a floodgate of tears from the stoic man. He rushed forward and wrapped his son in a bear hug, openly weeping with relief.

I shuffled my feet, feeling like an intruder witnessing an intensely private reunion. Three more kids, two boys and a girl, sidled into the room. They were older than Andrew, maybe a year apart in age. Their eyes were wide in shock as they beheld the brother back from the dead.

Despite my awkwardness, I was also proud. How could something like this be a sign of the apocalypse? We'd done something good here. Real good.

We said our goodbyes and stepped back onto the porch. Gareth wrapped an arm around my waist and kissed me on the forehead. "You're amazing," he murmured, pressing his lips against my skin.

I smiled at him, still shocked at how much had changed in such a short time, yet how much had stayed the same. I squeezed his hand. "Let's go home." He nodded, and we stepped off the porch.

Gareth opened a portal back to our trailer so I could change into my work clothes, then another to bring me behind Charlie's. It was early for dinner, but the parking lot was already filling up. The sun was beginning to set over the horizon, painting the sky in shades of pink and orange.

I pulled my apron tight as I walked into Charlie's, the familiar smells of fried food and stale beer washing over me. A few of Camden County's finest were parked on the barstools.

"Afternoon, gentlemen," I greeted them breezily, stopping to top off Deputy Jones' coffee. Ol' Jonesy lifted his mug in thanks, his bushy mustache dotted with flecks of black. I'd met Jonesy before. I used to know him as "Mustache," but our repeated interactions over recent months put us on a slanged-last-name basis.

"Thanks, Bloom. Can't ever have too much coffee."

I chuckled. "Amen to that!"

I headed behind the bar, nodding to Charlie as I tied my hair back. "How's it going?"

"Oh, you know. Same old soup reheated," he replied with a wink. Charlie was older than me and still cute in a grizzled kind of way. I knew he liked me. Grace, who worked the bar, told me as much. My love life was too complicated to entertain the possibility, though.

The crackle of a police radio interrupted my thoughts. "Unit Bravo, what's your twenty?" the dispatcher squawked.

Jonesy grabbed his shoulder mic. "Ten-nine at the grill," he replied. Police code for "on lunch break," I assumed.

The radio crackled again. "Be advised, we have a ten-sixteen at 452 Elm. Multiple ten-fifty-four-ds confirmed. Suspect at large. Requesting backup."

I froze. The address where we'd left Andrew. I didn't know what all those numbers meant, but given the expression on Jonesy's face, I knew it wasn't good. He and the other officers all stood. Jonesy glanced at me as he headed out the door. "Put our bill on the tab, will you?"

"Don't sweat it!" Charlie shouted over my shoulder before I could respond. "On the house."

With a nod, Jonesy hurried from the restaurant. My gut sank. Something happened to Andrew and his family. Had the old woman gone after him? Had she done something to Andrew's family?

I grabbed my phone, hands shaking. Gareth picked up on the first ring.

"We have a problem," I told him, voice low.

"What is it?" He sounded subdued. From my tone, he knew I was about to share grim news.

"Cops got called to Andrew's house. Multiple ten-fifty-fours, whatever that means."

"Shit," Gareth hissed. "That's dead bodies. Meet me outside. We need to get over there now."

"On my way." I ended the call and scanned the restaurant for Charlie. He was at the bar chatting up a customer. I caught his eye and mouthed, "Emergency." He nodded, and I bolted for the door. Charlie knew a little about what I'd been up to lately. He wouldn't tell a soul. He knew if I had an emergency to deal with, some kind of witch business, it was best he didn't get in the way.

I felt bad about it. Still, we were through the summer, and business was winding down now that tourists weren't flooding the lake area every weekend.

Gareth appeared out of thin air as my sneakers hit the gravel parking lot.

"What do you think happened?" I asked.

His jaw clenched, eyes cold. "I don't know, but we're going to find out."

I grabbed Gareth's arm as he traced his finger through the air. We would get there before Jonesy and the others like this. Everyone knew Gareth was a witch. But how could we explain *why* we were there when I'd just seen them at Charlie's?

"Wait," I stated. "We can't show up there out of nowhere. The cops saw me inside a few minutes ago. What will they think when I show up? You know how they are when witches are involved."

Gareth frowned but nodded. "You're right. Any evidence of witchcraft, and we're all suspects. I'll drop us a block away. We'll try to be discreet."

I nodded, biting my lip. We had to hope Andrew was safe and we hadn't made a horrible mistake in bringing him home. But the police scanner made it sound like the worst had happened.

After we arrived, appearing behind a bush about a block and a half south of Andrew's home, we saw flashing lights and crime scene tape.

Gareth shook his head. "We were here an hour ago. I can't believe all this happened so fast. The cops already secured the scene. That means…"

"Whoever did this must have come right after we left. They were watching us. Waiting for us to leave."

We crept closer, sticking to the shadows as we approached the house. Police cruisers and unmarked cars crowded the street. Neighbors stood on their porches or lawns, watching the scene unfold.

I sucked in a breath as we got close enough to see the front door hanging open. Small, bloody footprints led from inside the house down the steps.

Bile rose in my throat. Those weren't adult prints. Probably Andrew's.

"It looks like Andrew got away."

Gareth sighed. "If those are his prints. But did he escape, or did he…"

"No way. He wouldn't kill his family!"

Gareth's jaw was tight, eyes flinty. "We don't know what coming back from the dead does to someone. We can't rule it out, Briar."

Before I could respond, a cop emerged, guiding a sobbing woman to his cruiser. Andrew's mom.

My heart dropped, but I was relieved to see at least one survivor. She collapsed against the car, wailing. "My boy. He was home, he was alive. Andrew…something's wrong with him."

The cop shook his head, face grim. "Ma'am, your son died six months ago. I'm very sorry for your loss."

Six months? How could he have been dead that long?

Dread crawled up my spine. We'd made a horrible mistake. That thing we brought here, whatever it was, it wasn't Andrew. Or if it was, he wasn't himself. Not anymore.

When Mrs. Williams saw us, her eyes widened in horror. "You! Witches! You did this to him!"

Gareth and I exchanged anxious glances. "Ma'am, I swear, we did nothing to your son," Gareth assured her. "We found him in the woods and brought him home."

"There's a devil in my boy. A devil! And *you two* put it in him!"

The officer held Mrs. Williams back, but my gut twisted in a knot. Had Andrew killed his father and siblings? How did his mother escape? And how did a young kid manage to do something like that? His father was a big man. His siblings were older and stronger. All I knew was this must've happened fast, and something was wrong with Andrew. Was it something he brought back from the underworld? Had that witch in the woods done something to him?

Flashing lights and sirens approached from a distance. Jonesy and the others I'd served at Charlie's.

"We should get out of here," Gareth insisted. "This isn't going to go well for us."

I shook my head. "We have an alibi. Jonesy saw me at the restaurant."

"He didn't see *me*," Gareth reminded me. "You know how this goes, Briar. The cops aren't going to believe a twelve-year-old could do this alone, and we were the last ones who saw him."

I nodded. "Then get out of here. I'll talk to the cops. We need to know more about what happened in that house."

Gareth sighed. "I'm not leaving without you. But if they try to arrest me…"

"Then portal out of here. Whatever is going on here, I need you to help stop it. You can't do that if they put you in one of those damned cells."

Gareth nodded and put his arm around my shoulders. This wasn't the first witch-related crime the cops investigated. They had warded cells. Someone helped them set them up, though we didn't know who. They silenced a witch's magic. If they arrested

Gareth, he could get away. After they locked him up, he couldn't portal himself out of jail.

Gareth and I watched as the officer consoling Mrs. Williams took her aside. He was asking her questions. We couldn't hear what she replied from where we stood, but we needed those details. Whatever was happening, it was too much for the cops to handle. They didn't understand the scope of what we were dealing with.

If Andrew was somehow warped by his resurrection, what about the others? Maybe he went off the rails sooner because he was so young. If the others newly back from the dead started killing their families, we had to stop them. I didn't know how, but if there was any risk, we had to intervene.

Jonesy and the other deputies, who were with the county sheriff's department, exited their vehicles. Jonesy spotted me right away but didn't so much as nod to acknowledge me. He must've wondered why I'd come. I knew he'd have questions.

After briefly speaking with some of the other officers, Jonesy broke from the crowd and headed in our direction.

"Miss Bloom," Jonesy stated. "Mind if I ask you a few questions?"

I looked at Gareth. He nodded back. "I'll tell you what I can, but this is a mystery to me, too."

"Why don't you start with why you're here? I assume you overheard what was happening on my radio back at the bar?"

I nodded curtly. "Sorry, I knew the address. Gareth and I found Andrew in the woods. He'd come back from the dead, you know, like some of the other folks recently. We brought him home right before my shift."

"Did you see anything suspicious? Anything out of the ordinary?"

I shook my head. "There's nothing ordinary about bringing a dead kid back to his family. We thought we'd helped him, and they were happy. Beyond thrilled to see him."

Jonesy turned to Gareth. "What about you, Mr. Sharpe? You were there as well, correct?"

"I was, sir," Gareth confirmed. "Like Briar said, there wasn't anything strange at the Williams' home beyond what one would expect, given the circumstances."

"We met a woman in the woods," I piped up, not sure if it was wise to share this detail given her power. "She was a witch, I think. She found Andrew before we did. She tried to stop us from taking him back to his family. She said the boy was special. He had to be protected."

"Protected?" Jonesy tilted his head. "From what, exactly?"

"We're not sure," Gareth admitted. "That woman, she was powerful. If you'd allow it, sir, we'd like to investigate further. She's dangerous. She's more than you can handle, and I don't want to see anyone get hurt."

Jonesy raised an eyebrow. "How do you plan on investigating this matter further?"

"We have our ways." I gave him a cryptic smile. "Right now, we need to focus on what happened in that house. We have to find out what made Andrew attack his family."

Jonesy sighed. "I don't know what to tell you. We'll investigate, but things like this don't make much sense. We don't have all the answers."

"We understand that," Gareth replied. "We know things you don't, though. If you want to keep the people in this town safe, you'll listen to what we have to say."

Jonesy narrowed his eyes. "Are you threatening me?"

"No, we're not." I stepped forward. "We're tired of being treated like criminals every time something like this happens. We're not the enemy."

"You're witches," Jonesy stated matter-of-factly. "I'm not saying every witch is a suspect in every case like this, but you two were involved. Even if you weren't witches, we'd have to question you. You might have been the last people to see this family together before this went down."

"Are you saying we're suspects?" Gareth cocked a brow.

"Not yet, but we have to be thorough. That woman clearly thinks you two had something to do with what happened."

I thrust my fists on my hips. "She's confused. She's distraught. We were gone before this happened, and you *just* saw me at Charlie's."

"What about you, Mr. Sharpe?" Jonesy asked. "Where were you when this happened?"

Gareth sighed. "Back at Briar's place."

"Was anyone else there who can confirm your whereabouts?"

Gareth shook his head. "Aiden lives there, but he was working."

Jonesy glowered. "Don't leave town. Either of you. I'd advise you to steer clear of our investigation. I know you say you'd like to help, but the more you get involved, the more questions we'll have. Do you have a location in the woods where this woman supposedly had Andrew before you brought him home?"

"Maybe a quarter-mile east of the Brookside Cemetery where Andrew was buried. We discovered his grave was disturbed and went looking for him."

"Any reason you were wandering the cemetery, to begin with?" Jonesy asked.

I sighed. "Look, you know as well as anyone people have been coming back from the dead. That's not normal. We're concerned."

"We're investigating these resurrections," Gareth added. "This concerns the local coven as much as it does law enforcement."

I nodded curtly. Technically, Gareth wasn't the leader of the Morai coven anymore, but Jonesy didn't know that. "What Gareth said. Everyone's freaked out about these resurrections. This isn't normal, even for witches."

Jonesy rubbed his brow, reached into a pocket, and handed his card to me. "Keep me in the loop. I suspect we might need your help sooner rather than later. I'll do what I can to protect you from the investigation. But if you two get involved more than is warranted, if you get in our way, it will only raise suspicions."

"Understood." Gareth nodded. "We'll be careful not to overstep."

CHAPTER THREE

Jonesy shook his head and stalked off, leaving me and Gareth standing there like a couple of jackasses. I called after him, "Hey, we can help, you know!"

He didn't even turn around, the jerk. He'd told us not to get involved. He said he'd protect us if he could, but we didn't need protection. Honestly, the cops were the ones who should have stayed away. This was bigger than they were equipped to handle. Not like we'd convince Jonesy or any of the cops of that. He kept on marching to his cruiser, back stiff as a board.

Then his radio sounded. He retrieved it from his belt. I scurried closer to get a listen. "All available units, blah-blah-blah, a bunch of police codes, in progress at 2120 Oak Bend. Multiple victims, request immediate backup."

Son of a bitch. This wasn't just another day in our little slice of paradise.

Gareth grabbed my arm, his eyes wide. "Briar, that's—"

"I know," I interrupted through gritted teeth. We both recognized the address. It was where we'd brought back the first resurrectee. The fisherman Gareth had killed during his dark magic bender.

This was bad. Real bad. And Jonesy was too damn foolish to let us help. To him, we were lucky if we weren't suspects.

I tore after Jonesy, my boots pounding on the pavement. "Jonesy, wait!"

He didn't even slow down, the jerk. He grabbed his radio and barked, "10-4 dispatch, unit responding."

I caught up and grabbed his arm. "What the hell is going on? Talk to me!"

Jonesy shook me off, his expression stone cold. "Not your concern. I told you to stay out of this, Bloom."

"Like hell it's not my concern," I shot back. "Someone's killing folks out there, and it's obviously not us. We were here the whole time. This is more than you can handle. You need witches! You need us!"

"I don't need your kind of help." He turned away, dismissing me. "Now, get lost before I haul you in for obstructing an officer."

I wanted to scream. Gareth came up beside me, his eyes pleading for me not to make a scene. Clenching my fists, I took a deep breath. We didn't have time to argue. If we wanted answers, we needed to get to that crime scene before the cops arrived.

I met Gareth's gaze and nodded. He understood. In the blink of an eye, he grasped my hand, and we hurried behind a nearby shed. Gareth traced his finger through the air, and we vanished.

We reappeared in the woods outside the house on Oak Bend. The white picket fence was spattered crimson. Bloody footprints led away from the porch.

"Those aren't small prints," Gareth observed. "Not like the others. This wasn't Andrew."

My stomach turned to ice. Something in Andrew snapped earlier. Was the same thing happening to the others? If so, this wouldn't be the end of it. The second in a list of many bloody scenes, all likely associated with the resurrected dead.

I took off running, Gareth on my heels. Time to get some answers.

We burst through the front door and found the metallic scent of blood thick in the air. The living room was a massacre. Limbs strewn about, entrails spilling from gutted torsos. In the center lay a woman, eyes glassy, clutching a bundle to her chest.

I rushed over, Gareth right behind me. As I peeled back the blanket, bile rose in my throat. A cat, its head cleaved clean off.

"Oh god," I choked. A blur of red caught my eye. The cat's spirit. Its hue suggested it was a vengeful spirit. Best to keep my distance.

Gareth's face was stony. "It was Cyrus. The fisherman I killed last month."

I nodded, mind racing. We'd brought Cyrus back intentionally, hoping to give Gareth some peace for his crimes while infected.

"We need to find the others," I insisted. "Before this happens again."

Sirens wailed in the distance. Gareth grabbed my hand.

"We can't help them if we're locked up," he pointed out grimly. "Let's get back to the trailer. We'll regroup and figure this out."

With a flick of his wrist, we vanished from the grisly scene. My insides churned with dread about what we'd find next. Clearly, the dead weren't resting easy. If we didn't act fast, the living might not either.

We materialized inside my trailer, the abrupt change in scenery making my stomach lurch.

"Ugh, I hate teleporting." I groaned, steadying myself against the kitchen counter.

Gareth began pacing, raking a hand through his hair. "This doesn't make sense. The spell should've brought them back whole. Not…not like this."

I chewed my lip. "Well, Cyrus clearly didn't come back right. It's like he's feral or something."

"Why?" Gareth stopped, facing me. "What did we do wrong?"

I hesitated. The truth was, this resurrection spell was risky under the best circumstances. Using my Isis magic was like tinkering with a time bomb. I didn't really know what I was doing.

"Doesn't matter now," I finally told him. "We need to find the others before the police do."

I grabbed a map of the county and spread it across the kitchen table. X's marked where we'd brought resurrected bodies back.

"If Cyrus went home first, the others might too," I reasoned.

Gareth nodded slowly. "Where should we start?"

I traced my finger along the map, stopping at a house symbol.

"Here. Josiah Greene. He's nearest." I looked up. "If we hurry, we might make it before…"

I didn't need to finish. Gareth was already grabbing my hand, magic crackling at his fingertips. I steeled myself as the trailer blurred away.

Please, let us be in time.

The world spun back into focus, and I stumbled, clutching my stomach.

Gareth caught my arm, steadying me. We stood at the edge of a dirt driveway that wound through a thick copse of trees up to a small farmhouse. It was quiet. Too quiet.

I met Gareth's eyes. He gave a slight nod, and we moved toward the porch, magic at the ready. My heart pounded as we climbed the creaking steps. Gareth tried the door—unlocked.

He pushed it open, and I peered inside. At first, all seemed still. Then, my eyes adjusted to the dim lighting. Dark splatters on the floral wallpaper. A lone work boot lay in the foyer. Dread curled in my gut.

"Josiah?" My voice echoed down the empty hall. No response.

I stepped inside, Gareth close behind. The metallic tang of blood hung in the air. We moved through the living room, past overturned furniture. Toys scattered on the floor.

In the kitchen, we found them. Josiah's wife and two kids,

throats slashed, blank eyes staring. Gareth swore under his breath.

I blinked back tears, shaking. What had we done?

A floorboard creaked overhead. Gareth and I exchanged a look. Josiah was still here.

Without a word, we headed toward the stairs, magic crackling in our hands. Time to end this nightmare.

We crept up, wincing as the steps groaned under our feet. My senses strained, listening for any sign of Josiah. A faint shuffling sound came from down the hall. I met Gareth's gaze and nodded. We were ready.

At the end of the hall, a closed door. My heart slammed against my ribs. I took a deep breath and kicked it open, magic flaring.

Josiah stood hunched over the bed, bloody hands clutching at crimson sheets. I didn't know if there was a body in there, and I didn't want to look. He looked up, eyes feral, lips peeled back from his teeth.

"Josiah, stop!" I shouted.

He growled, dropping the child. Gareth flung a binding spell, but Josiah swatted it away like smoke. He lunged at us, hands outstretched.

I reacted on instinct, quickly slipping my Isis ring off my necklace and onto my finger. I didn't have a clue what I was doing. Before I could even think about what I wanted it to do, white-hot magic burst from the palm of my hand as if the ring already knew what I needed. I hurled it at Josiah. His body turned to ash, bones and all.

Panting, I turned to Gareth. His face was grim. "Are you sure that was wise? Using that magic again?"

I snorted. "Well, your spell didn't affect him. I had to do something."

"We have to tell Sydney." Gareth nodded. "She can rally the Morai, call in some other covens in the region. At the rate the dead are rising and turning homicidal, if we don't contain this soon…"

I glanced back at the pile of ash that was once a man. A man we had foolishly brought back. What had we done?

Without another word, we hurried downstairs. The dark deed was done, and we had to make it right again. Sydney wasn't as powerful as Gareth, but she had handled the Morai's affairs since Gareth resigned. They hadn't appointed a new leader yet, but she could reach out to other witches, and we needed every witch we could find.

CHAPTER FOUR

The Morai headquarters loomed before us, hidden behind its mystical veil. Only those with permission could see the old mansion that served as the hub for all magical operations in the area. Lucky for me, Gareth still had access, even if he was only a hedge witch now.

Gareth led me through the veil. I grabbed the iron gate, and it creaked open, revealing the wraithlike house. We hurried up the walkway, our shoes crunching on the gravel. The place was dead quiet. Too quiet.

We burst through the front door. The foyer was empty. No witches bustling around, no spellcasting. It was like everyone had up and vanished.

"Where is everyone?" I muttered.

Gareth and I hurried to Sydney's office. Her door was locked tight. Gareth whispered an incantation, and the tumblers clicked open.

We pushed inside to find an empty room. Well, except for a half-eaten bologna sandwich sitting in the middle of Sydney's desk.

"She must've left in a hurry," I remarked. "You think she got word of another attack?"

Those poor souls I'd resurrected for Gareth were out there somewhere with their humanity stripped away, nothing but violent killing machines. Not to mention everyone else who followed their lead out of the land of the dead, wherever that was, and came back in recent weeks.

If Sydney had raced off to stop one, she could be in real trouble.

Gareth's forehead creased with worry. "If my magic didn't work on the resurrected, the Morai might be in over their heads."

He was right. We hadn't been able to stop the undead creations with magic. Only my Isis power had worked so far. Brute force might do it, too. Chop them into bits. Like Sandy Claws in *The Nightmare Before Christmas*. Then again, that might not work. Their little pieces might put themselves together again like a liquid Terminator.

I pulled out my phone. "I'm gonna call Aiden. He might know where Sydney's at."

Aiden answered on the second ring. Before I could even ask about Sydney, I heard screaming and cursing in the background.

"Aiden?" I called. "You okay?"

"No, I'm not fucking okay!" he yelled. "I shot this undead motherfucker in the head like five times, and he won't go down!"

More screaming and gunshots echoed through the phone.

"Are you with Sydney?" I asked urgently.

"Yeah, she's here trying to magic these bastards, but it ain't working!"

I put the call on speaker so Gareth could hear.

"Aiden, tell Sydney to get everyone out of there," Gareth instructed. "Teleport them to safety. Only Briar has the power to stop the resurrected."

Aiden relayed the message, punctuated by more screams and

swears. Then he came back on. "Syd wants to know where to bring everyone."

Gareth suggested a few places. We'd be there shortly.

"Hurry," I added. "And stay safe."

I only hoped we could end this nightmare before anyone else got hurt. Sydney and the Morai were in over their heads, but with my unwanted Isis powers, maybe I could set things right again.

Not that I relished in it. Every time I used those powers, I risked losing myself. But lives were at stake. I had to do something.

"Aiden, where are you guys right now?" I asked.

More screams and gunshots in the background.

"Shit, I don't know!" Aiden yelled. "Some trailer park. The one with the toilet flowerpot on the porch."

I rolled my eyes. Standard yard decor in the Ozarks. It probably had a pink flamingo or two in the lawn as well. "Well, that narrows it down. Any landmarks? Street signs?"

"Uh, there's a Whirlpool washing machine on the porch. And a rusted El Camino up on blocks."

"Still not helpful," I uttered in exasperation. This was taking too long. People were in danger.

"Just get everyone out and text Briar your GPS location," Gareth suggested calmly. "We'll come to you."

"On it," Aiden confirmed. I heard him shouting to Sydney again, then the line went dead.

I anxiously paced as we waited for the text. Lives hung in the balance, and I was the only one who could end this. But using the Isis ring again terrified me. Those ancient memories threatened to overwhelm me and subsume me.

I'd have to be strong enough to maintain control. For the sake of the town I loved, hell, for the sake of the whole world, if the prophecy in the Book of the Dead was right, I had to master this power inside me. No matter the personal cost.

Finally, Aiden's text came through with the GPS coordinates. Gareth traced his finger through the air, grabbed my arm, and in an instant, we teleported directly to the scene.

I stumbled as we landed, nearly tripping over a lawn ornament built from a rusted-out tailpipe. Yep, this was the place all right.

Sydney and a few other Morai witches had thrown up a shimmering barrier around one of the resurrected, a large bald man with prison tattoos who snarled and threw himself against the magical wall.

"You're doing great!" Gareth encouraged Sydney as he added his own power to reinforce the shield.

The bald man's eyes glowed red with unholy light. This was no longer a man, more like a demon wearing human skin. I had to stop it before it could escape and wreak havoc.

My hand shook as I reached for the Isis ring on its chain. "I don't want to kill him," I admitted softly. "Maybe there's a way we can save him."

Gareth's expression was sympathetic but firm. "If we don't deal with him now, he'll kill others. It has to be done."

I swallowed hard. He was right. With trembling fingers, I slid the ring onto my finger, bracing myself as the flood of Isis' ancient memories surged into my mind. Images of pharaohs, other gods with animal heads, and Hebrew slaves building pyramids. I focused with all my will, pushing them back, clinging to my sense of self.

The resurrected man bellowed with rage, his body crashing against the magical barrier. I had to end this now before he broke free. A shield like that could hold a person, but this guy was more than met the eye. The fury in his eyes wasn't pure rage. It had a mystical source. I focused my power on him, visualizing him at peace, restored to his humanity.

Instead, his body exploded in a spray of gore.

I gasped, yanking the ring off my finger as if it had burned me. That wasn't what I had intended. More memories swirled through my head, and I squeezed my eyes shut, forcing them away.

"Badass!" Aiden whooped. "You turned that dude into lasagna!"

I shook my head and slid the ring back onto the chain around my neck, tucking it out of sight. I wasn't ready for this power. Still, ready or not, I had a destiny to fulfill.

"Anyone want to grab a Stouffers?" Aiden asked.

I stared at my foster brother. "You can't be serious."

"What? Them things are delicious. Take forever and a day to cook, but worth it."

Sydney tilted her head, running her fingers through her hair to pull out chunks of corpse. "I can't believe you actually want lasagna right now."

Gareth shook his head. "I'm never eating lasagna. Ever again."

"Let's get out of here." I cast one last uneasy glance at the carnage I'd created. I still wasn't sure I could control the ancient power of this ring, but I had to try. The fate of the world might depend on it.

Gareth put a hand on my shoulder, his eyes full of understanding. "It's a burden, I know. But we'll figure this out together."

I managed a small smile. Once, Gareth had succumbed to dark magic. Now he was one of the few people who truly understood the battle within me. With his help, maybe I could tame this wild power.

"Come on, I'll make us some tea when we get back," Sydney offered gently. Despite the gore in her hair, her voice was calm and soothing.

As we turned to leave, I caught a glimpse of the exploded body from the corner of my eye. Bile rose in my throat. I had done that with a flicker of power. What else was I capable of?

I shuddered. I would face it again soon enough. First, I needed rest…and screw tea. I needed a beer.

"We all need to clean up," Gareth stated. "Meet you back at Morai HQ in an hour?"

Sydney nodded and gathered the Morai witches. Aiden sauntered over to me. "This shit's getting bad."

"Why were you here to begin with?" I asked. "This isn't your fight, Aiden."

Aiden scratched his head. "Well, I can't let my woman go save the day while I'm flipping burgers."

I snorted. "Why not? Does she threaten your manhood?"

"Threaten it?" Aiden gasped. "No, she tickles it just right."

I chuckled. "Not what I meant."

Aiden bit his nails. Pretty gross, considering his skin was covered in dead guy. "I think I need a shower. I'll come with you. Besides, that Morai place is creepy AF."

Gareth raised an eyebrow. "AF?"

I grinned. "It's short for 'as fuck.'"

Gareth shook his head. "Well, that's lame AF."

"Is not!" Aiden stomped. "It's low-key legit."

I chuckled. "Aiden is trying to talk like kids these days. At his age, it's a little sus."

"Sus?" Gareth narrowed his eyes.

"Suspicious!" Aiden nodded matter-of-factly. "Come on, Gareth. You need to watch more YouTube. Get with the culture."

Gareth sighed. "I'll pass. We have bigger issues to deal with."

"Like dead fuckers!" Aiden exclaimed. "Talk about low-key sus!"

Gareth ignored Aiden's remark and put his hand on my shoulder. "Do you want to talk about what happened?"

I released a long breath. "Not really. All I want is a shower. I know I should, though."

He nodded. "That kind of power changes a person. I would know."

"It's not only the power," I admitted. "It's the memories. When I put that ring on, I get flashes of Isis' past. Thousands of years of history crammed into my brain all at once."

I rubbed my temples against the lingering ache. "It's too much. I can't control which memories surface. I'm not even sure they're real."

Gareth was quiet for a moment. "But you're resisting it. You're holding it off?"

I nodded sharply. "So far, but every time I do this, it's like the memories come flooding in stronger, clearer than before."

"Hey, I've got an idea," Gareth suggested. "Forget debriefing at HQ. How about we grab some beers and burgers at Charlie's instead?"

I smiled in spite of myself. "That sounds perfect, actually."

"It's beer-thirty!" Aiden grinned. "I'll let Sydney know. No one wants to hang out at that stuffy old house anyway."

CHAPTER FIVE

Gareth had hit the showers last and said he'd meet us at the bar shortly, so Aiden and I drove to Charlie's. I pulled into the lot and parked. The gravel crunched under my boots as I hopped from the truck, the familiar neon lights glowing through the dusty windshield. Aiden tumbled out after me, nearly face-planting into the rocks before catching himself.

"Whoa there." I grabbed him by the elbow before he took a nosedive. The big oaf only laughed, clearly three sheets to the wind already after chugging a six-pack while the rest of us showered. Couldn't take him anywhere, I swear. Not that I blamed him. After what he'd been through, not being a witch himself, he had to cope somehow.

Gareth appeared in a flash, materializing beside me without a sound. I jumped, startled. I should have expected it. Not that I wasn't used to his magic tricks, but I didn't expect him to show at that very second. "Christ almighty," I muttered, smacking him in the chest. "Give a girl some warning."

He winked, the cocky bastard. "Where's the fun in that?"

I rolled my eyes and headed for the door, the raucous sound of conversation and clinking glasses drifting into the parking lot.

As soon as we stepped inside, the familiar smell greeted me like an old friend.

"Well, slap me thrice and hand me to my mama!" Charlie hollered from behind the bar, waving a dishrag. "Y'all can't stay away, can ya? Bunch of gluttons for punishment."

I sidled up to the bar, Gareth and Aiden in tow. "Aw, you know you love seeing our shining faces, Chuck." I gave him a playful punch in the arm. "Ain't no place quite like home."

Charlie released a belly laugh. "Well, I'll be damned if you ain't right about that. What'll it be? The usual swill for you fine folks?"

"We're waiting on someone." I gestured toward a table, and Gareth and Aiden took a seat. "I think beers all around will do for now. Four pints of the good stuff."

Charlie laughed. "Well, what you mean by the good stuff isn't what I'd call it. I know you well enough, though. Four Coors Lights on the way."

Charlie grabbed four frosty mugs, filling them up from the tap. I brought them over to the table as Sydney breezed through the door, her long skirt swishing around her ankles.

"Thank goddess, I need this." She plopped down in the chair opposite me and took a long swig. A bit of foam clung to her upper lip, making her look like a kid with a milk mustache.

I leaned forward, elbows on the table. "All right, let's talk. What the hell are we gonna do about this mess?"

Sydney wiped her mouth with the back of her hand. "Well, we gotta stop 'em. That's for damn sure."

"No shit," I replied. "Except every time we put one down, two more pop up. It's like a goddamn hydra."

As if on cue, Charlie sauntered over, order pad in hand. "Well, well, Sydney Bell in the flesh. Ain't you a sight for sore eyes? What can I get ya?" His eyes lingered on her cleavage a little too long. Subtle as a freight train, that one. Thankfully, Aiden was equally entranced by his girl's bosom and didn't notice.

Sydney gave him a tight smile. "I'll have the chicken fried steak platter. With extra gravy."

Charlie turned to us expectantly. Gareth and Aiden put in their orders, cheeseburgers and fries all around. Charlie gave me a playful nudge with his elbow. "And for you, darlin'?"

I raised an eyebrow. "Since when did you become a waiter, Chuck?"

"I only serve the VIPs." He winked. "Top shelf clientele."

"Uh-huh," I returned dryly. "I'll have the garden salad, ranch on the side."

Charlie scribbled down the last order and strolled back toward the kitchen, leaving the four of us alone again. I turned my attention back to Sydney. "You were saying?"

She sighed in frustration, her fingers tracing patterns through the condensation on her mug. "If the damn resurrections don't stop, we'll be playing whack-a-zombie until kingdom come."

I took a long pull from my beer, the cold liquid soothing my dry throat. "And if it spreads beyond the region, we won't be able to keep up. We're falling behind as it is. And I sure as hell don't trust the cops to handle it."

Sydney sighed. "Well, someone has to say it. Gareth, if you didn't pressure Briar to use her power so you could fix your mistakes…"

Gareth leaned back in his chair, arms crossed. "We did what we had to do. What I did while infected by dark magic wasn't 'mistakes.' It was murder. I had to do what I could to make things right. I don't regret it."

"No?" Sydney challenged. "Seems to me you only made a bigger mess. And you put Briar in danger to do it."

I shook my head. "I make my own choices, Syd. I knew the risks. I worried about how using the Isis ring might change me, but that didn't mean I shouldn't try to save people's lives. We were talking about lives and families destroyed. It would have been selfish to refuse to do it out of fear when I could make things right."

Sydney shook her head. "It didn't make things right, did it? You brought them back so they could turn into cold-blooded killers. More people are dying because you did this than if you'd let the dead stay dead."

I understood Sydney's frustration. The resurrections had started after Gareth asked me to use my Isis powers to undo the deaths he'd caused while corrupted. But it wasn't his fault. Hell, it wasn't mine, either. We were both to blame. We'd dabbled with a power we didn't understand. We should have expected there might be consequences. Never in a million years, though, did I think this would happen.

"There's no point arguing over what's done," I stated evenly. "Casting blame now isn't going to save anyone. We need to focus on stopping new resurrections before this gets out of control."

Aiden chose that moment to release a truly epic belch. "'Scuse me," he mumbled, wiping his mouth with the back of his hand. He was working on his second pitcher of beer already, and his cheeks were flushed pink.

"Real nice, Aiden," Sydney sniffed.

"What?" He blinked at her innocently. "I'm getting my daily dose of probiotics."

I stifled a laugh. Leave it to Aiden to lighten the mood.

"As I was saying, we need a plan," I continued. "Preferably one that doesn't end with the whole county overrun by the walking dead."

Aiden perked up. "Ooh, I know! Flamethrowers!" He mimed blasting zombies. "Or we could lure them into the lake with brains on a fishing pole, then electrocute them!"

"Not helpful." Sydney sighed, though the corner of her mouth twitched. "Besides, where would we get brains, anyway?"

Aiden stared at Sydney blankly. "The morgue. Duh. Everyone knows that."

I took another swig of my beer, mulling over our options. None of them were great, but we had to do something before the situation spiraled out of control.

I wished I had a way to contact Dorian. He'd know what to do, I figured. If he didn't, maybe he'd learned something in Egypt that would help. He was off the grid, though. I'd tried his phone several times, and it always went straight to voicemail. I'd left him messages detailing what was going on, but so far, I didn't have any reason to believe he'd even listened to them.

Gareth broke the silence. "What if we called Balzac?" he suggested tentatively.

Stunned silence met the suggestion. Even Aiden stopped pretending to zap zombies with his imaginary flamethrower. Sydney looked at Gareth as if he'd suggested calling down fire from heaven.

"Why on earth would we call Ball Sack?" Aiden blurted, wrinkling his nose in distaste.

I could understand why my friends hesitated to call Balzac for help. He wasn't exactly our biggest fan. Still, I couldn't deny it might be a good idea. He was the reincarnation of Set and had knowledge of ancient magic and powers that far exceeded ours. If anyone knew how to stop these undead armies, it would be him.

"Look, I know he's no friend," Gareth stated. "What choice do we have, though? So long as we're responding to the murderous undead, they'll always be one step ahead of us. All we're doing is minimizing the damage, slapping a band-aid on the problem. We need a way to fix the veil between the living and the dead, to stop this whole problem before it gets worse."

"Gareth's right." I nodded solemnly. "We need Balzac."

At that moment, Charlie emerged from the kitchen carrying a tray with everyone's orders. He gave us all an awkward smile before setting our food on the table. Instead of leaving, he stayed nearby, lingering in the corner and listening to our conversation.

It made me uncomfortable, but I didn't say anything. Charlie had always had a crush on me, and perhaps this was his way of showing it. Then again, he'd seen his share of strange ever since Dorian showed up and I started embracing my witchy heritage. If anything, he was a concerned citizen.

I sighed and shrugged. "Maybe we don't have any other option." I continued, ignoring Charlie in the background. "We could try to summon Osiris again, or maybe Anubis, but that's risky in its own right since it's not clear what the gods really want. As much as we can't stand Balzac, calling him to help deal with the situation might be the best chance we have."

My friends all exchanged glances before slowly nodding in agreement.

"Okay," Sydney agreed hesitantly. "I guess I'll make the call. But if he screws us over…"

"I'm sure he will, one way or another," I told her. "I don't trust him, but Gareth is right. We can't keep playing from behind. We need to get ahead of this, and without more insight on how to stop the resurrections, more people will die."

CHAPTER SIX

I stabbed at my salad, shoving a forkful of lettuce into my mouth. The crunch was the only sound at the table as we all sat in tense silence, pretending not to notice Charlie hovering nearby under the guise of bussing tables.

Finally, Sydney pulled out her phone, keeping it low under the table like we were making some kind of drug deal. Her thumbs tapped out a quick text. A few seconds later, her phone buzzed, then it buzzed again. Not a text, but a phone call.

"Hello, Harold," Sydney stated. "Are you going to help or not?"

The whole table went quiet as Sydney listened to Balzac on the other end of the line. Whatever he was saying, she didn't like. Her face contorted in a dozen different ways as Balzac drawled through her earpiece. Sydney's eyes went wide, her nostrils flaring as she listened. She sucked in a long breath through her nose, then sighed louder than a hot-air balloon deflating.

"Fine," she grunted. "You were right, okay?"

I rolled my eyes so hard I swear I saw my brain. That damn Balzac. Like most men, the size of his ego was inversely proportional to the smallness of whatever he was packing in his drawers.

Sydney set her phone on the table with the speaker on.

"Fine, Balzac." Annoyance dripped from each word. "Briar and Gareth are here. They can hear you."

Balzac's smug laughter crackled from the phone. "I told you so. Now, admit it. I was right and you were wrong."

I slammed my fist on the table, rattling the silverware. "Right about what?"

"That without the knowledge of the gods, you'd be in over your heads." Balzac's smooth voice oozed with arrogance. "Face it, sister dearest, you need me."

My eye twitched. "Call me sister again, and I'll shove my boot so far up your—"

"Dear Isis," Balzac interrupted. "Are you really so afraid of remembering your past that you'd turn to me, your rebellious brother, to save the day?"

"It's Briar," I snapped. "Call me Briar."

Balzac chuckled. "I'll see you soon, sister."

The line went dead. I fought the urge to hurl Sydney's phone into the lake. That egotistical jackass was gonna drive me batty before this was all over. But damned if he wasn't right. We needed him.

The front door swung open so fast it banged against the wall, making me jump. Balzac strode in, wearing a shit-eating grin and his three-piece suit that probably cost more than my monthly salary.

Gareth narrowed his eyes. "Don't waste any time, do you?"

"Who needs airlines when you have magic?" Balzac grabbed a chair from another table and spun it around, straddling it casually. "I figured you'd call, given the circumstances. You know what this is, yes?"

I nodded, my stomach churning. "The Egyptian Apocalypse. We read about it."

"Quite so." Balzac leaned forward, steepling his fingers. "The dead will rise and rule the world. Unless the gods unite against it."

My palms grew sweaty. I knew what he meant.

"You must embrace your true self," he announced. "Become Isis once more. Put on the ring. Stop resisting."

I shook my head adamantly. "I won't lose who I am."

"We are the sum of our parts, dear sister," Balzac purred. "You need not fear. Isis' memories will only make you more."

His words twisted my gut. I didn't want to be more. I wanted to be me. Briar Bloom, small-town waitress. Yet the gleam in Balzac's eye told me I didn't have a choice. The apocalypse was coming, and my only hope was to become someone I barely knew.

Aiden banged a fist on the table. "Shut it, Ball Sack. That's my sister you're talking to."

Balzac threw back his head and laughed. "Isis is my sister, boy. My true sister. I know what's best for her."

Aiden's face turned red. He jabbed a finger at Balzac. "Fuck you, dude. She don't need your bullshit."

"Such language." Balzac *tsked*. "Unless Isis embraces her power, the dead will continue to rise. This town, this world, will fall. There will be no stopping it."

I chewed my lip, anxiety rising. According to Balzac, everything hinged on me becoming someone I wasn't. But if I didn't, we were all screwed.

Aiden scowled, arms crossed. "Don't listen to him, Briar. You're you. Ain't nothing can change that."

I wished I could believe that. However, with dead bodies piling up and Balzac smirking knowingly, the future felt more uncertain than ever. I had to make a choice, and whatever I decided would change everything.

Before I could respond, Charlie sidled up to the table, order pad in hand.

"Can I get you something?" he asked Balzac while trying unsuccessfully not to stare at me. Charlie had never been smooth.

Balzac ordered some fancy cocktail I'd never heard of, full of top-shelf liquors. Charlie hurried off to fill it.

Balzac turned back to me, eyes glinting. "I understand your hesitation, dear sister. This life is all you've known. But think of the power you could wield as Isis, mistress of magic and queen of the dead."

I shook my head. "The dead don't come back right anymore. They're killers now, not people." I shivered, picturing hollow-eyed corpses feasting on human flesh.

Balzac leaned forward, voice low and persuasive. "You could bring back your parents."

I pictured Mom and Dad alive again, laughing and hugging me. Then I imagined them as ravenous zombies. My stomach turned. "I won't put them through that torment."

"The dead are unfettered. They only act as they do because they lack a leader. The divine Isis could command them, as you did in millennia past."

I shook my head. "I don't believe you. What if you're lying to get me to do what you want?'

"But what if I'm speaking the truth?"

I rested my face in my palms. This was a lot to consider. If Balzac was right, I could access the power needed to control the dead. That wasn't the answer, though. He didn't say I'd stop them from rising, only that I'd be able to manage them. "This doesn't solve the problem. It doesn't stop the resurrections."

Balzac sighed. "The choice is yours, of course. But time is running short." He accepted his cocktail from Charlie with a thin smile. "I do hope you'll make the right decision."

I met Aiden's worried gaze. What I decided next would change everything. The weight of the world rested on my shoulders. And I had no idea what to do.

Gareth cleared his throat, breaking the tense silence.

"We know your real motives here." He glared at Balzac. "You want Briar to become Isis again so you can try to win her like you wanted before."

Balzac arched an eyebrow. "My reasons are unimportant. I simply wish to restore order among the dead."

"Bullshit," Gareth snapped. "You've always been jealous of Osiris. You want Isis for yourself."

Balzac's mouth curved into a cold smile. "Myths and legends. Believe what you wish, but I will only assist you if Isis returns." He turned to me. "Together, we can stop this, sister. We can defeat the darkness as we did eons ago."

My pulse raced as I considered his words. I didn't trust Balzac or his motives. But if he was right, embracing my past was the only way to save the future.

I took a deep breath. "Okay. I'll do it. I'll become Isis again." I met Balzac's triumphant gaze. "But I won't lose who I am now. Briar Bloom will still be here, too."

Balzac inclined his head. "Of course. We are all the sum of our memories. You will remain yourself, only stronger." He extended his hand. "So, do we have an accord?"

I hesitated only a moment before clasping his hand in mine. "We do."

Gareth shook his head, scowling. "This is a mistake. You can't trust him, Briar."

"What choice do I have?" I shot back.

Charlie approached and dropped the bill in front of me. He'd zeroed out the cost. Why even give us the bill if he was going to put it on the house? Then, I noticed a few scribbled words on the bottom.

Meet me back in my office. We need to talk.

I placed my credit card on the bill and handed it back to Charlie with a nod. Charlie left and went back toward his office. I nodded at the table. "I'll be back, guys. I gotta go check my shift schedule."

"Your shift as a waitress?" Balzac laughed, shaking his head. "You're the Divine Isis! These mortals should serve you, not the other way around!"

I shook my head. "I told you, Balzac. I'm Briar. I'm a waitress. That will never change."

CHAPTER SEVEN

I stepped into Charlie's office, leaving Balzac and his cryptic bullshit with Gareth, Sydney and Aiden. When I entered, I saw a pile of clothes—Charlie's clothes—and a big golden retriever sitting in front of his desk, panting away with its tongue lolling out.

What the hell?

"Hey boy, whatcha doing here?" I moved to pet the dog. His fur was soft, and he leaned into my hand, tail thumping on the floor. "Did you eat Charlie or something? Bad dog! Charlie ain't kibble!"

The dog looked at me with those big brown eyes and panted more. Then, all of a sudden, its form blurred and contorted right before my eyes. Fur melted away to reveal bare skin, and the dog stretched and changed until Charlie stood there in all his naked glory.

"Jesus H. Christ!" I yelped, slapping a hand over my eyes. "What the fuck!"

"I've been meaning to tell you…"

"You dog! Put some damn clothes on, Charlie!"

"Briar, I—"

"I'm calling HR for sure!"

Charlie only chuckled as I heard him rustling around, grabbing his clothes. "We're a small town bar and grill, Briar. I *am* HR. I'm sorry for the shock. I didn't know a better way to tell you."

I risked a peek through my fingers to see he at least had underwear on now. "You couldn't say, 'Hey Briar, I've got a secret. I'm a part-time dog?'"

Charlie stared at me as he slipped on his jeans. "I'm not a dog."

"Barks like a dog, humps your leg like a dog, call it a dog."

"I never humped your—" Charlie sighed and scratched the back of his head. "I'm a man, Briar. I have abilities. It's personal. You're the first person I've told outside my family in years."

I grunted. "So, what then? You're a shapeshifter?"

"Not exactly." He buttoned up his shirt. "I can shapeshift. That's among my abilities. Technically, I'm a druid. A little out of practice, but it's what I am."

"A druid?" I lowered my hand fully now that he was decent. "Heard of druids, don't know what they are. Is that like some kinda witch or something?"

"I suppose you can say that. Your magic comes from a Coptic lineage and tradition. Mine is Celtic." Charlie sat behind his desk, mercifully fully clothed. "I've been a druid my whole life. It's in my blood."

My mind was spinning faster than a Tilt-a-Whirl. Magic and myth were leaking out all over this Podunk town lately. "So, if you're a druid, how come you never used your powers to help us out before? You knew we were knee-deep in shit with the Grand Coven and the Réminians before that. Plus that fight with Jim Bob Anderson, may the devil damn his soul. You could have done something."

Charlie shrugged. "First, my abilities aren't really suited for fighting. I try not to use them. I suppose I'm something of a hedge druid. There aren't any others around so far as I know, and I like to keep to myself."

I nodded slowly. "Like a hedge witch. Got it." Seemed Charlie had been holding out on us. But why?

Charlie held up a hand. "Before you get upset, let me explain. Druids have always worked in secret to avoid interference from other magical organizations like the Morai and the Grand Coven."

"Why would the Grand Coven screw with you?"

Charlie sighed. "The druidic philosophy is different than other magical traditions. Most witches believe they use magic. It serves them. For us, it's exactly the opposite. To subject ourselves to oversight by other witches would compromise our core values."

I crossed my arms, tapping my foot. "Okay, so why reveal yourself to me now?"

"Because I don't want you making a mistake," Charlie told me earnestly. "I've been observing for a while now. Things don't add up with Balzac's story. If he's really an ancient Egyptian god, why isn't he trying harder to stop the dead himself? Instead, he wants you, a young, barely trained witch, to take on the powers of Isis?"

I chewed my lip. "Well, maybe only Isis can fix this. If I'm really the goddess reincarnate, it's not like I'm taking on something new. If I get those old memories back, I'll know how to use my power. I won't be a novice anymore."

"Perhaps," Charlie conceded. "I suspect Balzac has other motives. If the end times concern him so much, he should fight it himself. Unless he wants it to happen." His eyes bored into mine. "What if becoming Isis makes things worse instead of better?"

My pulse quickened. I didn't know what to believe anymore. Sensing my distress, Charlie removed a bracelet from his wrist and clasped it around mine.

"This will guard your spirit," he explained. "It was my father's and my grandfather's before him. It's been in my family for generations dating back to the pre-Christian era. Basically, it grounds you, keeps outside forces from influencing your mind and soul."

I examined the simple pewter band. "How's it work?"

"It was originally meant to protect the wearer from faeries." At my skeptical look, he added, "They're not Tinkerbell. Faeries walk between worlds, some with dark intents. This bracelet forms a barrier around your essence."

I shook my head. "We're not dealing with faeries here. We've got Egyptian gods and walking dead."

"Doesn't matter the threat," Charlie revealed. "It will still shield you. If you really are Isis, if accessing her power is truly innate, it won't stop that. It should keep you grounded and focused. On the other hand, if the ring is infecting you with something external, this will block it."

I let his words sink in. "So you think I'm being possessed or something?"

"I'm not sure. Look, I'm no sage. I barely practice my druidry and haven't studied your brand of magic. What I do know is my bracelet should help you maintain control either way." Concern filled his eyes. "I don't want you losing yourself." Charlie paused a moment and took a deep breath. "I don't want to lose you, either."

"Charlie, I—"

Charlie shook his head. "I know you don't feel the same way about me, Briar. It's fine. You're special, though. Something about you has captivated me since the first time you stepped through my doors and asked for an application."

I glanced at the bracelet again. "You're a good guy, Charlie. A great friend."

Charlie pressed his lips together. I didn't mean for the f-word to be so stinging. No guy wants to be friend-zoned by a girl he likes. "I'm here, Briar. I'll help however I can. Even if all you need is someone who will listen."

I took a deep breath. "I might take you up on that. It's hard talking about all this with Gareth or Sydney. Gareth has been sweet since Dorian left, but he doesn't really get me. Not completely. He doesn't see *me.* He only sees the witch he grew up thinking he'd marry someday. Aiden, well, he makes a joke of it all or says something ignorant. He doesn't understand."

Charlie stood and approached me. He put a hand on my shoulder and looked into my eyes. "I get it, Briar. I know how it feels to be different, to have everyone around you not understand who you really are. You're not alone. You have me, and I won't let anyone hurt you."

I felt a warmth spreading through me as Charlie's words sank in. His unwavering support was exactly what I needed in this crazy world of magic and gods. I smiled, feeling a sense of gratitude and affection for my friend.

"Thank you, Charlie. You have no idea how much that means to me."

Charlie smiled back at me, and I felt a flutter in my chest. Maybe there was something more between us.

I quickly pushed that thought aside. Bigger things were at play, and I couldn't afford to let myself be distracted.

I unfastened my necklace and slipped my Isis ring off the chain. "I'm going to try this with you. I don't want to give Balzac an opportunity to screw with me when it happens. If Isis takes over…"

Charlie nodded, his expression serious. "I understand. I'll be here to help you. Let's do this together."

I took a deep breath and closed my eyes, holding the ring tightly. I focused on my breathing, feeling the weight of the bracelet on my wrist as it grounded me. Slowly, I felt a warmth radiating from the ring, spreading through my body. Images flooded my mind, memories that weren't mine but felt familiar and ancient. I saw pyramids and temples, heard the whispers of priests and the chants of worshippers.

Then, suddenly, I was standing in a vast desert, the sun

beating down on my skin. Before me stood a towering figure, a god in human form, with the head of a falcon. Horus. Somehow, I knew who he was the moment I saw him. He looked down at me with eyes that seemed to pierce through my being.

"Briar," he stated, his voice deep and resonant. "Welcome."

My mind flooded with thoughts. The ring still worked. That meant I wasn't possessed. I really was Isis. Or was I?

"You used my name. You didn't call me—"

"Isis?" Horus chuckled through his beak. "That's who you were, once. You are more than that now. Who we are always changes. We grow through our experiences. Your human life has a greater influence on who you are than your lives past."

"You're my son. I remember now."

Horus nodded. "Yes, I am. And I am here to guide you, to help you access your power and fulfill your destiny."

My heart raced and swelled as I gazed at the god before me. I felt a mother's love I'd never known in my human life. It was like a dream, but at the same time, I couldn't shake the feeling something wasn't right. "What if I don't want to fulfill my destiny? What if I want to live a normal life?"

Horus' expression softened. "I understand why you might feel that way. You've become human. Your dreams and aspirations are different than they used to be. Perhaps, Mother, that's exactly what's required. Your humanity is not a weakness. It's the source of your true power, a strength you can use to do what you couldn't or wouldn't before."

I tilted my head. So many ancient memories. My mind couldn't accommodate all of them at once. When I thought back, I recalled what I used to be like. "I wasn't a very good mother, was I?"

"You were what any mother of the gods would expect you to be. As I said, you're more now. The old Isis wouldn't have risked everything to save humanity. Briar Bloom will."

I snorted. "Well, you're not human. No one worships you anymore, or me for that matter. Why do you care?"

Horus stepped closer to me, his eyes still piercing. "Do you really think the gods only care about worship? We may not demand it as we once did, but we've changed through the centuries. Through the witches, the netters, who wield our power. At least, some of us have. We see your struggles, your pain. We see the darkness that threatens to consume your world. Some of us want to help."

"Some of you?" I took a deep breath. "Set is here. Reincarnated in some balding dude named Harold Balzac. I don't trust him, but I think I need his help."

"Set has no desire to save the world, nor does he care to see it end. Set only thinks of himself. He may be an ally, to a point, so far as it serves his interests."

"And his interests…I know the mythology. He wants me, but, you know. Ew."

Horus shrieked a laugh. "He's changed less than you'd think despite taking human form. When you rejected him before, he tried to kill Osiris out of envy. You must tread carefully. He may help you, but your friends aren't safe. Especially if he thinks history is repeating itself. If you choose someone else over him."

I shook my head. "That's why he wanted to break up me and Dorian before."

Horus nodded. "He knew with Dorian by your side, you would be stronger and less likely to turn to him for help. He wants to isolate you, to make you rely solely on him. I know you've grown closer to the other warlock. The more you let him in, the more Set will conspire against him."

I sighed. He was talking about Gareth. Seriously. Could my love life get any more complicated? Dorian, then Gareth, now Charlie, and freaking Balzac with a *Fatal Attraction* level obsession? I'd always been the weird but cute girl. The kind who guys flirted with when no one was watching but didn't give the time of day in the company of their friends. In this wacky world of witchery, though, I was the freaking *Bachelorette*.

"So, I can't get too close to anyone. I have to lead Balzac on enough so he'll help me stop the freaking apocalypse, but not so much he'll lose his shit and destroy the world himself if I reject him."

Horus nodded. "Yes, you must be smart and strategic. You have the power to choose your own path, Briar. You are not bound by fate but by your own decisions. Choose wisely."

I furrowed my brow. "You said this is my destiny."

Horus nodded. "You were destined for this opportunity to stop the end of the world. How you go about it, if you do at all, remains your choice."

I took a deep breath, feeling the weight of the world on my shoulders. I also felt a renewed sense of purpose and determination. I was Briar Bloom, and I was going to save the world.

"I will." I looked at Horus. "Thank you for your guidance."

Horus smiled, his eyes shining with pride. "You are a goddess, Mother, but you're also a human, Briar. Never forget that."

With those words, the world faded, and I felt myself pulled back to reality. When I opened my eyes, Charlie was still beside me, holding my hand.

"Did it work?" he asked, his voice tinged with concern.

I curled my lips into a deviant smirk. "I am the Divine Isis! Bow down, kiss my feet, or die!"

Charlie gasped and took two steps back, almost falling over his desk.

I couldn't help myself and burst into laughter. "I'm screwing with you, dude. I'm still me."

Charlie released a sigh of relief and chuckled. "Don't do that, Briar. You nearly gave me a heart attack."

I looked at my hand, and the ring had lost some of its luster. It had completed its purpose. My past-life memories, my power, were now a part of me. Charlie's bracelet hummed against my wrist, a subtle vibration. Had it really protected me? Was that why my old memories didn't overwhelm my humanity? It was hard to say, but I wouldn't take the bracelet off. Probably not ever.

"What happened when I was gone?" I asked.

Charlie tilted his head. "You were gone? It only took like a second. Maybe two. You drew in a sharp breath, your eyes glossed over, then you were back and wanted me to worship your feet. I hate to tell you, Briar, but I'm not a foot guy."

I shook my head. "Well, damn. That's a deal breaker, Charlie. You know I can't be with a man who won't give my tootsies the love they deserve."

Charlie grinned. "Wait. So you're saying you do have feelings for…"

I raised my hand. "Don't go there, Charlie. I was joking with you. The truth is, what I learned when I put on the ring is that I can't get close to anyone. Not without risking their lives."

"What really happened to you?" Concern filled Charlie's face.

"I'll just say I have to work with Balzac to save the world. If I let anyone else get too close to me, well, he's not exactly stable."

Charlie nodded. "I understand. Don't worry, Briar. Like I said, I'll be here for you, no matter what."

I smiled as a sense of gratitude washed over me. Charlie was a good friend, always there to support me. I couldn't get too close to him, either. Not if I wanted to keep him safe.

"Thanks, Charlie. For everything. I think this bracelet might have been what I needed. And your support, of course."

"I'll be here, like always. If you need me, you know where to find me. Whatever is going on, I believe in you."

I tilted my head. "I might need a few shifts off."

Charlie sighed. "Of course. I understand. Come back to work when you're ready. You'll always have a job. If you need any extra money or whatever to stay afloat, I'll loan you what you need."

I shook my head. "I appreciate that, but I'm not a charity case."

"Oh, it's not charity, Briar. I said it's a loan. You can pay me back with future wages."

Charlie winked at me. I laughed. "Of course. That will help."

"Come on," Charlie urged. "You'd better get back out there before your friends come looking for you."

CHAPTER EIGHT

I approached the table, my heels clicking on the sticky floor of Charlie's. The gang was still there. Gareth, Sydney, Aiden, and that snake Balzac. As I got close, Balzac's beady little eyes lit up when he saw the Isis ring glinting on my finger.

"Isis!" He jumped up and wrapped me in a bear hug before I could react. I swallowed the bile rising in my throat and forced a smile, hugging him back. "Set," I stated through gritted teeth. "You expect me to embrace you after you murdered my husband?"

I was playing the part I knew, and with all those memories in my mind, it wasn't hard.

"I only did it out of my love for you!" Balzac insisted. "That was ages ago."

"Indeed it was," I bowed my head. "We have larger issues at stake than the petty vengeances of times past."

I glanced at the others as Balzac finally let me go. Gareth and Sydney looked concerned, while Aiden seemed confused, as usual. "It's time to get to work," I announced.

Balzac clapped excitedly. "Oh yes, my queen, it is time!" He grabbed my arm. "Let us go forth and destroy those who would stand against us."

I pried his hand off me. "Whoa there, trigger finger. We can't just start blasting them. I may have my mojo back, but I can't even sense where they are."

Balzac pouted but nodded. "Briar Bloom is still a part of you. You speak like her."

I bowed my head. Yeah, I'd lost focus. Needed to get back into my Isis role. "As you said before, I've lost nothing. I am myself, but I'm also the pitiful girl who used to work this bar."

"Used to?" Aiden raised an eyebrow.

I shrugged. "I quit. A goddess can't serve tables."

Technically, Charlie let me take a leave of absence. But I was playing a role.

Aiden looked genuinely hurt and worried. Like someone had punched him in the gut. "And you ain't pitiful, Briar. You're badass. You're my sister! I love you!"

Balzac licked his lips. "Yes, son. I'm in love with my sister as well."

"Not like that, you sicko!" Aiden thrust out his chest. I was afraid he would try to fight Balzac, which wasn't a fight my foster brother could win.

"Ignore him." I glanced at Balzac. "The ways of mortals and those of the gods are as different as night from day."

"You are wise as always." Balzac placed his chubby hand on my lower back. I wanted to grab it and twist it off his arm.

"Damn straight," I remarked. "We have no time for this petty nonsense. Tell me, Set, how do we begin? I do not sense the presence of the dead."

Balzac nodded. "Without Anubis to help, we shall have to track them the old-fashioned way. First, dismiss these measly humans so it can be us. So we can enjoy one another as only two gods might!"

I forced a laugh. "Oh, Set, there will be time for such things later. We need these humans to witness our power so they can spread word of our might."

Gareth and Sydney shared another look. Aiden shook his head. "I ain't worshipping my sister, crazy or not."

Balzac moved to slap him, but I caught his hand. "Patience. These are modern humans. They are not accustomed to the ways of the gods. They must come to worship us of their own accord."

"You're right, of course," Balzac replied. "I am too quick to anger. Lead on, my radiant Isis, and I shall follow."

I tried not to cringe at his fawning. I needed to play along a little longer. I hoped we'd take care of this matter quickly. I'd sort out how to fix the veil between the living and the dead, and I'd feel comfortable enough with my power by that point to put Balzac in his place.

As we spoke, more old memories zapped in and out of my mind. It was all there, although I couldn't focus on any single memory at once. Eventually, I suspected, it would be second nature. Surely I'd remember something I could use against Balzac when I stopped needing his help because I sure wasn't going to become his boo.

"Let's be off then," I announced. "Time is short, and there is much work to be done."

We headed out into the muggy night air, my heels clicking on the sidewalk. The others trailed behind, radiating unease.

"Where to first, my love?" Balzac asked. "Point the way, and I shall smite any who stand against us."

"Patience, Set," I counseled again. My old abilities were still intact. I suspected they were part of Isis' abilities from the beginning. Short of stealing a police scanner, the spirits of the forest offered the best chance we had to track down any resurrected homicidal folk. "All in good time. For now, we must attune ourselves to the restless spirits."

I stretched out my arms and closed my eyes, calling to the animal spirits of the surrounding forest. I allowed myself to open up mentally and feel around for any foreign energy. As if on cue, more spirits than usual flooded from the forest outside and around Charlie's. Hundreds, then thousands only visible to me, rushed toward me to answer their mistress' call. Some were small, some large, but all seemed eager to help in whatever way they could.

Two spirits emerged in front of the others, the two who'd been the closest to me since I was a girl. It was Roy, my spirit-wolf, and Smokey, my spirit-bear. They were both huge now, and their presence filled me with warmth. I welcomed them both with open arms and thanked them for coming.

Roy bowed his head in respect while Smokey nuzzled against my leg. I felt how much they cared for me even without speaking. It was like a warm blanket wrapping around my soul.

"Thank you," I told them softly. "I'm so glad you've joined us."

The others seemed to understand my connection with these two animals and stepped back to give us space as they waited patiently by our side.

"You are my eyes and ears!" I announced. I knew Gareth, Sydney, and Aiden couldn't see them. I wasn't sure if Balzac could or couldn't, but they knew what I was doing. I might have looked like a batty lady talking to people who weren't there, and they didn't realize how much stronger my connection with the spirits was now, but they trusted me to figure it out. Sort of.

They trusted Briar, anyway. I wasn't sure if they trusted Isis. At some point, I needed to let Gareth know I was still me. I couldn't let Aiden know, though. He'd do or say something to spoil my ruse.

"Between all of you, you've seen everything. Show me, in your minds, any who've returned to their bodies and where I might find them."

Yeah, the animal spirits could show me their own memories. An ability I'd only realized now that I had, something I'd never done before. It was pretty awesome. As Isis, I might not have been an omniscient deity, but when the dead spirits of the wild were my eyes and ears, I was as close to all-knowing as anyone could be.

The spirits moved, swarming around me in a dizzying display of color and light. I felt their presence in my mind, each a unique energy I could easily identify. Their memories, their witness of the dead and resurrected, twisted around my fingers like snakes. The spirits had given me their knowledge, and I felt the information pouring into my mind.

I took a deep breath, feeling the weight of responsibility on my shoulders. I had the power of a goddess at my fingertips, and I needed to use it to protect those around me. The spirits had shown me what I was looking for. Now, it was time to act.

I opened my eyes. "Let's go. We've got a lot of ground to cover."

CHAPTER NINE

Spirits of every shape and size danced through the trees, their whispers guiding me toward the risen dead. They were feeding me image after image, memory after memory. My mind couldn't handle it all. It was too much. I was still trying to sort through all my new memories from Isis' past. I rested my right hand over Charlie's bracelet on my left wrist. It grounded me. It helped me focus, but it was still a lot to deal with. My head was spinning, but I was still myself. At least for now.

I picked my way over roots and under branches, trying to discern the best place to start. Go to the graveyards and deal with the most recently resurrected first? Or intervene in those already risen who'd returned to their families? It was only a matter of time before they turned murderous if they hadn't already.

As I pondered where to start, I noticed Gareth leaning against a tree, looking like he'd stepped off the cover of Witch Weekly. His eyes met mine for a second before darting away. Was he nervous?

I couldn't blame him. He didn't realize I was still myself. I'd played the role of Isis well to satisfy Balzac.

Aiden and Sydney sat on a large boulder beside Gareth.

Meanwhile, Balzac was prancing about the woods like a fool, giggling.

I gave Gareth a subtle grin and a nod. I added a wink for good measure. Relief washed over his face, and he smiled back. Message received. I was still me.

Gareth sidled up beside me, keeping his voice low.

"I'm nervous about all this," he admitted. "Feels like we're being set up."

I rolled my eyes. "Was that an intentional Set pun?"

He shrugged. "Maybe."

I nodded and glanced at Balzac as he frolicked between the trees. "We're definitely being set up. I have a plan, though."

I lowered my voice to a whisper, making sure Balzac was out of earshot.

"I've been thinking more about my memories as Isis. Set is the god of chaos and confusion. Trying to understand his motivations is pointless because there's no order to anything he wants. He only wants to sow mayhem. He gets off on it. If it ends the world, so be it. He doesn't care either way."

I met Gareth's eyes, my expression serious. "He's obsessed with Isis, too, so do yourself a favor and keep your distance until this is over. If he thinks you're making a move on me or decides you're competition, he'll turn against you."

Gareth nodded, brow furrowed. "Is there a way we can stop him?"

I chewed my lip. "Actually, yes. After Isis resurrected Osiris, well, he came back dismembered."

Gareth raised an eyebrow. "Dismembered?"

I nodded. "Set stuffed him in a box and tossed him into the Nile. A fish ate his…member. He came back and couldn't reproduce the normal way. Apparently, as Isis, I used my power to impregnate myself. Not sure how that worked. It's a little weird. Some kind of telepathic intercourse. Whatever."

Gareth chuckled. "I'm sure the answers are there if you probe your memories."

I nodded. "It's not important. That's how Horus was born. Eventually, Horus challenged Set's rule over Egypt through a series of trials and overcame him at every turn."

Gareth's eyes lit up with understanding. "You're saying if we challenge Set…"

"We can beat him," I finished. "The key is understanding his nature. He thrives on disorder and revels in mayhem. If we strategically introduce more chaos into the situation, we can use his own appetite for anarchy against him."

"How do we do that?" Gareth asked.

I chewed my lip, thinking. "I'm still working that part out. Going through these memories is like searching a library for one specific book. It's in there somewhere. I just have to keep looking." I rolled my eyes. "Whoever organized this mental library needs to be cursed. The Dewey Decimal system sucks."

Gareth laughed, his eyes crinkling at the corners. "Let me know if I can help with the search. I'd be happy to grab some books off the shelf for you."

I smiled. "I'll let you know. For now, keep your head down and pretend to worship Set like the others. An opportunity will present itself. Chaos always contains the seeds of its own destruction."

Gareth nodded, his expression growing serious again. "I'll do whatever it takes to stop that monster."

Balzac sauntered over, his beady eyes narrowed in suspicion. "What'sss this?" he hissed, baring his teeth as if they were fangs. "How dare a pathetic mortal speak with the Divine Isis!"

I suppressed an eye roll. "Calm yourself, Balzac," I replied smoothly. "The boy was merely pledging his loyalty and singing my praises, as is proper."

Balzac scrutinized Gareth, who bowed his head submissively.

"Y-yes, your grace," Gareth stammered. "I live only to serve you and the divine Isis."

Balzac sniffed, mollified. "See that you remember your place, worm." He turned to me, expression softening. "Come, my dear, walk with me. We have much planning to do."

He extended a chubby hand. I forced a smile and took it, allowing him to lead me deeper into the shadowy forest. Gareth fell into step behind us, head still bowed.

Balzac led me in a skipping dance between the trees, following the flickering shapes of spirit animals, which he could apparently see, too. I let him guide me, gritting my teeth each time he pulled me closer.

"Soon, the resurrected will be ours to command," he crowed, his breath hot on my neck. "Together, we will raise an army the likes of which this world has never seen! All will tremble before us."

"Yes, my love," I replied through clenched teeth. "It will be glorious."

He squeezed my hand painfully, his sharp nails digging into my skin. "You cannot imagine how I've longed for this day, my queen. For us to be together again, side by side, ruling over these pathetic mortals."

I swallowed a scathing retort and forced another smile. "As have I," I lied.

As we continued, Balzac babbled gleefully about conquest and chaos. I only half-listened, focusing instead on the memories and knowledge filtering back into my mind. Horus had defeated Set before by revealing his true chaotic nature. If I could somehow push Balzac into tipping his hand too soon, he might sabotage himself again.

First, I had to play along and lull him into complacency. The opportunity would come. I only had to bide my time. For now, we had to stick to the task and deal with the resurrected dead.

That meant focusing on the influx of information flowing into my mind from the spirit animals around us.

An image of a man, grave dirt still clung to his open-backed suit and caked under his nails, appeared in my mind. He was on the doorstep of what I assumed was his former home. If his family was inside, they were in for a rude reunion.

"I know where to start," I told Balzac before turning to the others. "Come, follow me. It's time to begin."

CHAPTER TEN

I snapped a twig under my sneaker as we trekked through the brush, the crack echoing in the stillness of the forest. My heart thumped against my ribs, adrenaline flooding my veins even though we hadn't encountered anything threatening yet. This whole resurrection nonsense had my nerves frayed worse than a cut-rate sweater.

Behind me, I heard a rustle and whipped around to find a golden retriever peeking out from some brambles. Charlie. That damn fool would get himself killed, traipsing after us like a lost puppy. I should've known he couldn't resist playing the hero.

I turned back around, pretending I hadn't seen him. Maybe the others wouldn't notice if I didn't make a fuss. I'd have to find a way to shake him when we reached the house. Throw him a bone or tell him to scram back to his bar before he ended up as Set's chew toy.

Gareth strode ahead like a warrior on a quest. Balzac slithered behind him, scowling at the back of Gareth's perfect head. More issues were piling up between them than on a table in a doctor's office waiting room.

Gareth knew to mind his Ps and Qs. He was on board with

the plan. But Balzac remained a wild card. It was hard to anticipate the actions of someone who craved only chaos. The only thing predictable about Balzac was that he'd be unpredictable.

I swatted a mosquito off my neck, my nerves buzzing louder than its wings. We had to end this, and soon, before Lake of the Ozarks turned into the Lake of the Undead. I prayed Charlie didn't get his fool self killed before we could send these corpses back to the dirt where they belonged.

We arrived at the house faster than I'd anticipated. We couldn't teleport via Gareth without losing my connection to the spirits. I wanted to keep that flow of information coming. At any moment, if an undead person snapped and went homicidal, we needed to be ready to go. Until then, we'd follow whatever leads I could pick up.

The house I'd seen in the animals' visions looked as I expected, its weathered siding and sagging porch emerging from the gloom like an apparition. It sat back from the road, obscured by towering oaks dripping with Spanish moss. A narrow gravel drive led past it to a rickety dock on the lake, where an aluminum fishing boat bobbed on the murky water.

I held up a hand, signaling the others to hang back. "I'm going in solo first. These poor souls don't know what's happened to them. I don't want to trigger this man's rage. He may be less likely to snap if I approach him alone."

Balzac scoffed. "Oh please, Isis. Enough with the bleeding heart routine. We both know you're useless without me." He slithered up beside me, a sinister grin spreading across his face. "Shall we?"

With a resigned sigh, I turned the handle of the warped wooden door. It creaked open into a dimly lit living room, the air heavy with mold and stale cigarette smoke. A figure still caked in grave dirt hunched by the soot-stained fireplace. His head snapped up, bloodshot eyes narrowing.

"Who the hell are you?" he growled, tightening his grip on the rusted fire poker.

I held up my hands in a calming gesture. "Be at peace, friend. We mean you no harm."

The man's face contorted in confusion and rage. Behind me, Balzac released an exaggerated sigh.

"Oh, for Ra's sake, Isis. Allow me." He glided forward, eyes flashing. "You belong to us now, worm. I am Set, god of chaos and war, storm and sky." He gestured at me with a flourish. "This is Isis, goddess of magic and fertility. You will bow to us!"

The man's eyes widened in shock and fear. So much for treading carefully. I expected the man to snap. After a moment, he slowly sank to one knee before us, head bowed.

Balzac shot me a smug grin. "See? That wasn't so hard."

I rolled my eyes. "Yes, bravo. This doesn't solve the problem at hand. We can't possibly track down every resurrected soul before they start butchering innocents."

Balzac waved his hand dismissively. "Why should we care? A little carnage adds spice to the monotony of human existence. We're still building an army, one undead soul at a time."

I stared at Balzac, stomach twisting. This was not going according to plan.

"We can't let them slaughter people unchecked," I insisted. "As gods, it's our duty to guide and protect humanity."

Balzac snorted. "You've gone soft, Isis. Too much time among the mortals has diluted your resolve. What does their suffering matter, so long as it furthers our glory?"

I shook my head firmly. "I won't stand for innocent bloodshed. There must be another way."

"Would a human hesitate to kill a field mouse or stomp on an ant?"

I shook my head. "That's different."

"It is not. We are as far superior to these naked monkeys as they are to insects."

I snorted. "You're reincarnated into a human body, as I am. You seriously mean to tell me you care nothing about them?"

"Of course I care about them!" Balzac crossed his arms. "Like a rancher cares for a herd of heifers. They are here to serve our purpose. There's no reason to cultivate a heart merely to let the herd graze."

"We're talking about lives here, Set. Things aren't like they used to be. I'm not the only god who has changed," I told him as I recalled Horus's words. "Others feel as I do."

Balzac paced around the room. "Tell me, Isis. Do you remember what it was like at the height of our glory?"

I narrowed my eyes, doing my best to tap into the goddess' old memories. "I do. We were never as great as we thought. We forced the people of Egypt to obey and to honor us, and we trained the netters to do our will. We enslaved foreign people to build monuments to our chosen pharaohs."

"Yet eventually, our people fell," Balzac cut in. "They forgot about us, and other gods took our place. It wasn't because we weren't strong but because we'd grown complacent. I won't make that mistake again."

I shook my head. "You're delusional, Set. Even the gods of the Greeks, though later adopted by Rome, fell. Ultimately, a single god whose followers preached compassion prevailed over us all."

Balzac waved his hand through the air. "Tell me, dear Isis, how has that fared in history since? This god of compassion, revered by millions, is honored among some of the most arrogant that humanity has ever produced. A compassionate deity breeds a rebellious and prideful people. Humanity craves submission. They want and need to be ruled. We're here to fulfill their deepest desire."

The man on his knee looked between us uncertainly. "I honor you both."

"See." Balzac ruffled his fingers through the man's hair as if he was a dog. "Only those who die can come back and know their place. This is what must happen to all of them. They must all die and rise again. This is our purpose."

"To kill everyone?" I shook my head. "That's madness."

Balzac shrugged. "Their deaths are temporary. They must die, their bodies with their pride. Then, they will live again. Happiness isn't found in imagined freedom. Humans can only be happy when they serve. When they worship their betters."

I narrowed my eyes. I should have known better than to bait Balzac into this debate. Even my ancient memories protested against his words. I couldn't push it, though.

"We'll discuss this further," I told him. "Perhaps you're right."

"Of course I am!" Balzac laughed.

I turned to the man with a gentle smile. "What's your name, friend?"

"G-George," he stammered.

"Stand up, George," I pronounced. "You're coming with us."

He climbed to his feet, poker still clenched in one dirt-caked hand. I studied him sadly. We may have delayed this one man from violence, but countless others were out there, and we couldn't reach them in time. Balzac didn't care if they killed people. The more who died, the more who could come back and worship his pompous ass.

George shuffled from the house behind us, poker still in hand. As we emerged into the moonlit yard, Gareth, Sydney, and Aiden came into view near the tree line.

Aiden's eyes widened as he took in George's filthy, bedraggled form. "Hey man, I know you! We had algebra together sophomore year. How've you been?"

George fixed Aiden with a hollow glare. "I've been dead, asshole."

Aiden put his hands up, affronted. "Whoa, no need for name-calling. I was only making conversation. Why you gotta be a dick about it?"

At the word 'dick,' something in George seemed to snap. With a feral growl, he reared back and swung the iron poker at Aiden's head.

Aiden yelped and dodged just in time. The rusted metal tip grazed his cheek and left a bloody gash.

"George, stop!" I shouted. Magic I hadn't intended to channel amplified my voice. "You will not harm these people. Stand down, now!"

George froze mid-swing, the fire in his eyes dimming to confusion as my command overrode his violent impulse. The poker dropped from his fingers to thud dully on the dirt.

Meanwhile, Sydney was already at Aiden's side, tracing a healing spell over the wound on his face with her finger.

"We gotta get you some anger management classes, buddy," Aiden suggested to George with a nervous chuckle.

I sighed, gazing sadly at the dazed resurrectee. Controlling them was the easy part, but we weren't any closer now to stopping this undead apocalypse. Clearly, Balzac had no intention of helping us do that, either.

I turned to Balzac, who was watching the scene unfold with an amused smirk.

"See, Isis? Your pathetic human morality makes you weak," he stated. "Allow me to kill the boy. He's not your true brother. I am! He'll rise under our command and be ten times more useful than in his current state."

Anger flared in my chest. "That's not happening."

"Isis! You're only delaying the inevitable. We cannot stop the end. It's been foretold in the Book of the Dead! The only question is if these dead who rise will rule beneath us or apart from us. You've seen what they'll do without our guidance."

"Enough!" I snapped. "I don't want to hear another word of this 'kill them to save them' bullshit. It ends now."

I saw the stubborn defiance in Balzac's eyes, but he held his tongue. We'd continue this argument later, I was certain.

For now, I turned my attention back to George. The grave

dirt was flaking off his skin and clothes, revealing pallid flesh and dim eyes. He stared at me, awaiting direction like a wind-up automaton.

My heart broke for him. For all of them.

"George," I told him gently. "You cannot harm other people. I forbid it."

He blinked slowly, processing my words. Then, with a guttural cry, he grabbed the fallen poker and plunged it into my stomach.

I gasped, more shocked than hurt. My divine thrall had failed. George was beyond reason, consumed by feral rage and pain.

As my vision darkened, a golden blur shot from the tree line. Charlie, still in dog form, leaped at George with bared teeth.

Charlie's jaws clamped down on George's arm, violently shaking as he tried to wrest the poker away. George howled, smashing at Charlie with his free hand.

"Enough of this," Balzac snapped. With a flick of his fingers, a bolt of magic sizzled through the air. Charlie yelped as the energy coursed over his fur, forcing him back into human form.

He crouched there, naked and disoriented. I wanted to run to him and explain, but the pain in my stomach kept me pinned against a tree.

"Well, well." Balzac sneered, looming over Charlie's hunched form. "It seems we have a druid in our midst."

Charlie glared at him defiantly. "I serve the balance. Nature itself. Not you."

"Such confidence for one so exposed." Balzac's smile turned cruel. "I could end your life with a thought, whelp."

Charlie's jaw clenched, but he held Balzac's gaze. "Then why haven't you?"

Balzac laughed. "I admit, you intrigue me. A druid could be useful."

He extended a hand to help Charlie stand. Charlie refused to take it and stood on his own.

"Charlie?" Aiden shook his head. "I can see your wanker, dude."

Charlie didn't respond. He fixed an enraged gaze on Balzac. "We'll stop you. One way or another."

"Will you?" Balzac laughed. "Come with me, Isis. Leave these foolish mortals to their trifles. We have work to do."

I pushed myself between Charlie and Balzac. "You will not harm my friends. You will stop this madness. Need I remind you I've defeated you before?"

"Correction," Balzac stated. "Your poor excuse for a son stopped me. I've learned my lesson. Besides, you don't have the balls he did. Fight for them if you'd like, but soon they'll die with the rest. Then, you'll have no choice but to stand at my side."

I shook my head. "This isn't over, Balzac. We will stop you."

Balzac narrowed his eyes. "Isis! Call me Set!"

I shook my head. "Call me Briar, asshole."

My power welled up within me in proportion to my anger. Magic tingled on my fingertips. Before I could release it over Balzac, he waved his hand in a flourish and disappeared.

"Shit." I shook my head. "So much for thinking he'd have answers."

"He has answers," Gareth countered. "He doesn't want to share them. But you can access Isis' memories now, Briar. The answers we need must be buried in your mind somewhere."

I drew a deep breath. "Sorting through those memories isn't as easy as you'd think. If I have the answer, it's not coming to me."

"Then perhaps I can help," Charlie added, covering his bits with one hand. "There's an ancient practice. I haven't used it since I was a child, but it can help you access suppressed memories."

Gareth shook his head. "All this time, there's been a druid under our noses, and we didn't even know it. I'm not sure I trust your magic, Chuck."

Charlie shook his head. "My magic is not violent. It's healing.

It's your magic that's dangerous. The kind that tries to manipulate reality to accomplish your purposes."

I clenched my fists. "First, Charlie, go get some damn clothes. Gareth, we need his help. If there's a way I can remember how to stop this, we have to find it. I trust him."

"You trust a druid who has lied to you for years? How long have you known this man, Briar, and never had a clue?"

I shook my head. "It doesn't matter. He had his reasons. Considering how you're speaking to him when he intervened and risked everything to help me, I can see why."

Charlie glanced at my blood-soaked shirt. "You're injured, Briar."

I tilted my head. "Oh yeah." Then, I raised the bottom of my shirt. Blood stained my skin, but there was no wound. "I think I healed myself."

Sydney approached and touched my stomach. "Wow, Briar. I can feel the power inside you. It's amazing."

"It is," Gareth added. "Very well, the druid can help. I confess I don't know how this power you have works. If he can help you, what do we have to lose?"

CHAPTER ELEVEN

Balzac was gone. Set was building his army, and he had his first recruit. The bastard who was supposed to be obedient but stabbed me with a damn fireplace poker instead. If Balzac thought he could control these undead bastards, I suspected he was in for a rude awakening. George paid us homage at first, but it didn't take long for him to turn from reverence to rampage.

Charlie's voice cut through the chill settling over the clearing.

"To tap deeper into your past life, we'll need a stone circle for the ritual. If we were in the UK, it might be easier to get to one. Here, we usually have to build on an as-needed basis."

Sydney, Gareth, and I exchanged knowing glances. "I know just the place," I told him. "Dorian's old sanctuary in the woods by the bar. It's already got a stone circle."

Charlie tilted his head. "Why does Dorian have a druid's circle?"

I shrugged. "He used it to channel his magic. He allowed me to use it to amplify mine back when we were hunting down Gareth."

Gareth snickered. "That was Darth Gareth, thank you very much."

Sydney chuckled and backhanded Gareth on the arm. "You're such a nerd."

Gareth's jaw dropped. "There's nothing nerdy about *Star Wars*. It's cool! They use the force. Did you know the netters in Egypt were sometimes called Djedi? We are the modern-day Djedi. That's where the Jedi came from in those movies. Since I went to the dark side for a while, it's not inappropriate to refer to that version of myself as Darth Gareth."

"I like it!" Aiden piped up. "I'll be the captain. Beam me up, motherfuckers!"

Gareth regarded Aiden with more seriousness in his eyes than was warranted. "You're talking about *Star Trek*. I'm talking about *Star Wars*. You can't mix them up. It's a sacrilege."

Aiden snorted. "Who the hell stuck a lightsaber up your butt? Head to the medical bay, buddy. You'll need to see Dr. Crusher to have that removed."

Gareth sighed. "You did it again."

Aiden shrugged. "Did what? Who cares if they're trekking or warring? They're both Star-whatever. It's all the same shit."

I raised my hand to silence Gareth before the urge to defend the integrity of *Star Wars* against *Star Trek* overtook his better sensibilities. "Can we stay on task, boys?"

Gareth bowed his head. "Sorry."

"Me too. Hey, while we're on the topic, I have a serious question."

Gareth sighed. "What is it, Aiden?"

Aiden scratched the back of his head. "What is a Captain's Log anyway? Is that what happens when Captain Picard uses the shitter on the Millennium Falcon?"

I clasped my hand over my mouth as Gareth turned three shades of red. I cleared my throat and knew I would have to force a subject change before Gareth was lured back to the Dark Side of the Force. "We were talking about Dorian's stone sanctuary."

Gareth drew a deep breath, then shook his head. "Dorian has

been a hedge for centuries. Stone circles aren't usually a part of our practice, but general stonework is. The pyramids, for example. My guess is Dorian encountered druids at some point and coopted their practice."

Charlie shrugged. "Well, I can't say for sure if it will work. It's been a long time since I did anything like this. Haven't actually worked with a stone circle since I was twelve. Part of coming of age in my family. If it works, it should help focus your thoughts, Briar, so we can journey deeper into your past life's memories."

Gareth grimaced. "Well, we should get going. Dorian left his wards up before he left, so I can't teleport us there."

Charlie waved it off. "No worries. We'll hoof it back to the bar first. Gotta check on things and make sure we have enough staff on the clock to take off for a few hours more. Then we'll take a nature hike, conjure ourselves a past life or two."

Gareth teleported us to Charlie's parking lot in a blink. When we materialized, I saw Deputy Jones' cruiser parked out front.

"Shit," I muttered. This was the last thing we needed.

We headed inside, the little bell above the door announcing our arrival. Jonesy sat at the bar, nursing a soda and chatting with Grace. When he saw us, he set down his drink and stood.

"Evening, folks," he announced in that casual yet authoritative way cops had. "Mind if I have a word?"

"Sure thing, Deputy," Charlie replied smoothly. "What can we do for you?"

Jonesy's gaze ticked over each of us before settling back on me. "I have some questions about these resurrection cases occurring around town. I told you to steer clear, Miss Bloom. Why am I finding evidence that you're connected to a number of these cases? Too many to be a coincidence."

I kept my face neutral, but my heart kicked into overdrive. How the hell did he know?

"Evidence?" I asked, unable to keep the edge from my voice. "Who the hell has evidence? Someone snitching or something?"

Jonesy's lip quirked. "I'm afraid I can't reveal my sources. However, you and Mr. Sharpe here seem to be present at a number of the scenes."

Aiden shook his head. "It's those damn doorbell cameras, ain't it?"

Jonesy tilted his head. "Well, I can't—"

"Yup," Aiden added. "Doorbell cameras. You'd think y'all would put them to good use, like catching UFOs and shit. Instead, you use them to cheat."

"Cheat?" Jonesy asked. "How are we cheating?"

"Because it ain't fair to the criminals if you have camera evidence anywhere!" Aiden insisted. "Like, how can they compete with that?"

"You think it ruins the competition between criminals and the police?"

Aiden nodded matter-of-factly. "It's all about balance. Superman would be a big spandex-wearing bully without Lex Luthor. Batman would be a real jackass if there was no Joker or Riddler to give him good crime-fighting competition."

"I'm not sure I'm following your logic, son."

"Balance!" Aiden insisted. "You know, like yang and yin. Day and night. Hot and cold. Hot chicks and ugly people. Everything needs its opposite. It's what keeps the universe together. That's what Sydney says."

"That's not exactly—" Sydney stopped herself, realizing there was no point trying to explain. She'd probably tried to teach Aiden about how witches view the world, and he'd reduced it all to the balance of hot versus ugly females.

"Think about it," Aiden continued. "How would I know Sydney was hot if I never saw any ugly people? You know, to know the difference. Ugly people are important. If it wasn't for them, I wouldn't appreciate Sydney for the beautiful person she is."

Sydney narrowed her eyes. She was trying to think how to

respond but was at a loss. "Aiden, I think you're kind of missing the point. Why don't we let the deputy here do his job?"

"It's not only that!" Aiden continued to rail, ignoring Sydney's plea. "Those doorbell cameras ruin CSI TV shows, too. It's not as interesting when they solve every other case because some dumbass walked in front of someone's house."

Jonesy furrowed his brow. Then he turned away from Aiden and back to me. "The point is, Miss Bloom, you've been investigating these cases as witches. I thought I made it clear this is homicide first. Until we've done our job, you can't get involved. If you do, I won't be able to protect you. Hang around these strange cases too much, and it won't take some of my colleagues too long to suspect the witches nearby are probably responsible."

I cleared my throat. "We're trying to help, Jonesy. If you saw us, you know we were only trying to stop the dead from hurting folks. It's a complicated situation."

"It's an ongoing investigation into multiple homicides," he replied coolly. "Interfering could mean obstruction charges."

I threw my hands up in exasperation. "Fine, charge me, then! This is bigger than a few murders, Jonesy. We're talking end of the world big. So, if you want to arrest me, go ahead. But at least let me save the goddamn world first!"

Jonesy's eyebrows shot up in surprise. Clearly, he hadn't expected that response. I was done playing games, though. I met Jonesy's gaze steadily, challenging him to make the next move.

Jonesy held my gaze for a long moment, his expression unreadable. Around us, the bar's chatter continued obliviously. Finally, he sighed and rubbed a hand down his face.

"All right, Miss Bloom. I can see there's more going on here than meets the eye," he conceded. "I know you've always tried to do right by this town. So I'm choosing to trust you on this…for now."

I released a breath I hadn't realized I was holding.

"Thank you, Jonesy. I know it's asking a lot."

He nodded grimly. "Keep me updated if anything else happens." He hesitated. "If you see cops on the scene, leave before people ask too many questions. And for god's sake, avoid doorbell cameras."

"Got it. Will do, Deputy!"

Jonesy tipped his hat and turned for the door. As it swung shut behind him, I sagged against the bar in relief. That had been too damn close.

"Well, that was exciting," Charlie deadpanned, appearing beside me to collect empty mugs. "If we're going to do this, I need a little help. Aiden, care to man the grill?"

"Sure thing, boss."

Sydney stepped up. "I can wait some tables. I've waitressed a few times. Sort of comes with the territory when you're trying to pay your way through a law degree."

Charlie nodded. "You're hired."

I nodded at Sydney and mouthed, "Thank you." She winked back at me. When I first found out she was dating Aiden, I had to admit, I was skeptical. She was a Morai witch and intelligent, not to mention beautiful. Aiden was handsome enough, but why would an educated girl give a guy like Aiden the time of day?

It took me a while to figure it out. What Aiden lacked upstairs, he made up for with his heart. He was sweet. He'd do damn near anything for me, as his sister, and just as much for Sydney. Hell, he'd risk his life for pretty much anyone.

He didn't have any magic at all. Truth be told, though, I'm not sure if any of us would still be alive if it weren't for Aiden. More than once, he'd risen to the occasion. It didn't take a lot of bravery to do his job, to man a grill, but it was needed at the time.

"Come on," I told Charlie. "I'll show you the way."

CHAPTER TWELVE

The damn cicadas were screaming so loud I thought my eardrums would burst. Didn't help that the humidity was thick as pea soup, either. Sweat trickled down my back as I led Charlie and Gareth through the woods, swatting mosquitoes away every few steps.

Up ahead, those spirit critters fluttered between the trees again. Squirrels, songbirds, more deer than I could count, all transparent and glowy. They'd be creepy to anyone else, but to me, they were beautiful, their presence comforting. They seemed happy I was there.

"We close?" Charlie asked, huffing. The path twisted on forever.

I glanced back, lips curled in a sly grin. "Can't keep up, old man?"

Charlie chuckled. "I'm not that old! Besides, if I wanted to, I could become an eagle and fly ahead. If I knew where I was going."

I tilted my head. "You can fly? That's cool."

"Yeah." Gareth rolled his eyes. "He can become a bird. What a pecker."

Charlie glowered at him. "For your information, eagles don't really 'peck.' They devour."

I chuckled. "Behave, boys. I'd really like it if you two could get along. If we do this, I'm not sure what it will be like. Tapping into old memories from some past life as a goddess. I've barely scratched the surface, and what little I've managed to access is overwhelming."

"Heaven forbid," Gareth chuckled. "You're going to remember what it's like to be worshipped as a goddess. Must be tough!"

I flipped him off, making him laugh. We all knew I wasn't too thrilled about this past life regression crap. But if it helped stop the apocalypse…

"Right over this ridge," I announced. We crested the hill, and there it was. The stone circle, nestled amongst the trees. Massive slabs of granite standing over ten feet tall, encircling a clearing. I'd seen plenty of pictures of places like Stonehenge, but this was different. Magical.

Memories already charged the energy of the place. Where Dorian and I kissed the first time. The nights we spent under the stars. The first time I realized my abilities were more than a quirk, that I was actually a witch and cast a few spells.

"Hot damn," Charlie whispered. "Ain't nothing like this anywhere this side of the Atlantic. It's almost like this place was lifted right from the British Isles and dropped in the Ozarks."

I drifted toward the center, fingers trailing along the weathered boulders. Power thrummed under my touch. "Dorian made this place. I'm not entirely sure how he did it. He has a unique connection with forest and water spirits."

Charlie joined me in the circle and started unpacking a knapsack of supplies he'd retrieved from his office back at the bar. Candles, incense, crystals. He arranged them carefully around the perimeter while I stood awkwardly, not sure what to do.

"Have a seat right there in the middle." Charlie motioned to a flat stone.

I sat cross-legged, trying to calm my nerves. Gareth lingered at the edge of the trees, giving me an encouraging smile. I drew a deep breath and closed my eyes.

The flutter of wings made me open them again. Little blue lights danced amongst the trees, spirit animals that had followed us from the bar. I grinned. Having their energy around always gave me courage.

"All right, let's begin." Charlie lit the candles. Their glow softened the shadows. "I want you to relax and open your mind. Let my voice guide you into a meditative state."

I closed my eyes once more. Charlie began a low chant in a language I didn't recognize. The sound wrapped around me, soothing and rhythmic. I felt myself sinking deeper like I was floating in warm water.

Then, a wave of energy rippled through my body. I gasped softly. It was Charlie's magic, resonating with my own, blending together. An image took shape in my mind. A tall, regal woman with dark hair and kohl-rimmed eyes. Isis. Myself, from another life.

I stared at Isis, transfixed. The image sharpened, and suddenly, I was no longer in the stone circle. I stood in a golden wheat field, the sun warm on my face. I didn't see Isis ahead of me. Now, I was Isis. Her eyes were mine, but I wasn't in control of my actions. I was in my own mind like a spectator. In the distance, I saw the Nile River glittering.

Isis bent next to a wooden box on the riverbank. With a jolt, I realized it contained Osiris' remains. This was the moment when Isis had brought her beloved back to life.

I watched as Isis began channeling her magic. I knew that power. The air shimmered with magical energy. It was the same power I'd used when I'd raised the dead before. Slowly, Osiris emerged from the box, resurrected.

Minus an important organ between the legs. A fish had gotten the worm. That part was gone forever.

That wasn't the strangest thing. His face was blank, devoid of any features. I couldn't manipulate Isis' eyes to squint and focus more. I could only see as she saw, and for whatever reason, she didn't react in any way that suggested she was shocked.

It wasn't that Osiris's face was gone. More like it was blurred, absent from my memory. He certainly didn't appear in his natural form, the way I'd encountered him before. This was in the flesh, in a body mostly like a man. Then again, perhaps the animal head came and went. Yes, that was it. I remembered now. Why was his face blocked from my memory?

All I knew was it couldn't have been by accident. Someone had altered that memory, prevented it from being passed along through whatever whacked-out realm my spirit floated across between my prior life and this one. Or, maybe someone had wiped my mind after that. Before I realized who I used to be in a past life. Perhaps I didn't want to remember. Was his loss so painful on a subconscious level I erased his face from my memory as a defense mechanism?

All a bunch of theories. Any one of them could be right, or none of them. It was strange, though. Someone, whether myself or someone malicious, didn't want me remembering what Osiris looked like.

His appearance was only part of the issue at hand. I saw my hand grab Osiris' as an energy enveloped them both. A crowd gathered around, all tracing strange geometric patterns through the air. Different ingredients were brought forth and cast back into the river from which Isis had drawn Osiris.

Then the river burst with power into the sky, forming a wall as high as my divine eyes could see.

We were sealing the veil. Raising Osiris broke the veil between life and death, as I'd done when I resurrected Darth Gareth's victims. At the time, I hadn't recovered the memories to know what I was doing, the consequences that would follow, or how to fix it.

The problem? This ritual to fix the veil was more complex than the power Isis used to resurrect Osiris. Far more complicated. It involved dozens of magicians, Djedi, and Egyptian netters. After they deposited the ingredients into the river, the two gods—me and Osiris—combined their power to cast it.

The vision faded. I was floating back up through layers of consciousness. With a gasp, I opened my eyes. I was sitting in the stone circle again, my heart pounding.

I had seen the secret to repairing the veil and stopping the apocalypse. Now, I had to figure out how to make it happen. Something told me Balzac wouldn't make it easy.

I inhaled deeply, trying to steady myself after the intense vision. The stone circle hummed with residual energy. I glanced at Charlie and Gareth.

"You all right there?" Charlie asked, his brow furrowed in concern. He could always tell when I'd had a rough spellcasting sesh.

"I'm good." I got to my feet shakily. The spirit animals were still fluttering amongst the trees, their presence reassuring. "It was intense, but I saw what I needed to see."

"So you know how to fix the veil now?" Gareth asked eagerly, stepping closer.

I nodded. "I saw how Isis did it when she resurrected Osiris, but I'm not sure we have the resources needed to pull it off."

"What do we need?" Gareth asked.

"Well, I saw several ingredients native to Egypt," I explained. "Things like red sandstone and the oil of a Terebinth tree." I paused, counting off more items on my fingers. "We'd also need magic from at least twelve Djedi as well as the power of another god added to mine." Unless any Djedi and gods were running around willing to help, that might not be possible.

Nothing ventured, nothing gained, right? I looked at Charlie and Gareth.

"Any ideas, guys?"

Gareth pinched his chin. "The Morai are basically the descendants of the netters, the Djedi. Sydney can gather enough of the coven to help. The ingredients shouldn't be difficult, given my ability to teleport. Finding another god who is willing to help? Well, Set clearly won't do it. Any chance you could summon Osiris or talk to Horus again?"

I dragged in a breath. "Maybe, but Osiris was incarnate when he did it. I can't tell you how, but that was a necessary part of it. The spell has to be cast using a single front from one side of the veil. In other words, it must be a god reincarnated like me."

Gareth scratched his head. "But not Set."

"How many gods are there walking the earth?" Charlie asked.

I sighed. "We don't know of any others. How do we even go about trying to find another reincarnated god? I didn't even realize who I was until I put on that ring. I might never have learned of my past life otherwise."

Gareth tilted his head. "Perhaps we can reach out to some of our brethren. It stands to reason that if there's another god or goddess in the flesh, he or she is among our witches. It's a matter of figuring out whose abilities might stand out, like yours did, suggesting they're something more. Something unique."

Charlie paced around the circle. "Does the god have to be Egyptian?"

I shrugged. "Not sure. I mean, I sort of assumed. I don't know why or why not."

"If you cannot find any of your Egyptian deities reincarnate, I might know someone from my Celtic tradition."

I interrupted Charlie. "Wait, are you saying there's a chance we could use a Celtic deity to help fix the veil?"

Charlie nodded. "Yes, a few come to mind. The Morrigan, for example, is known for her ability to control fate and death. She could potentially help us with this task."

Gareth furrowed his brow. "Would she be willing to help us?

We don't exactly have a good track record with the deities we've encountered so far."

"It's worth a shot," I stated. "We can at least try to reach out to her and see if she's willing to lend her power to our cause."

"Okay," Charlie replied. "I can send a message to my contacts in the Celtic community and see if they know of any possible reincarnate deities. I can also try to make contact with the Morrigan and see if she's willing to help."

I smiled. "Thanks, Charlie."

"I'll do the same," Gareth added. "Sydney and I will reach out to other Coptic witches and see what we can find out. I'll also work on gathering the necessary ingredients. Teleportation helps."

"What about me?" I asked. "I need something to do!"

"Want to go wait on a few tables?" Charlie asked.

I snorted. "Not really. Still, it beats sitting on my ass waiting for you guys, or waiting until Balzac does something bad, or some dead guy goes homicidal."

Charlie laughed and slapped me on the back. "That's the spirit! Let's head back to the bar. You can relieve Sydney, train her, or whatever, so she can go with Gareth. I'll need some time in my office to reach out to my contacts."

CHAPTER THIRTEEN

The hazy glow of neon beer signs and dusty track lighting greeted me like an old friend as I pushed through the tinted glass door and walked into Charlie's. Sydney stood behind the bar, her blonde hair frizzing out every which way like she'd stuck a fork in a socket.

"Oh, thank goddess, you're here." She wiped her hands on a rag. "This shit isn't easy. It makes my contract law classes seem like child's play."

Grace winked at Sydney. "Don't be so hard on yourself. You did great!"

Sydney laughs. "Thanks, Grace." She turned back to me. "That woman is a gem."

"Hey, Syd," Gareth called. "Come with me. We have work to do back at Morai HQ."

"Says who?" Sydney cocked her head. "Lest you forget, I'm in charge there now, you dirty hedge."

Gareth laughed. "Yeah, yeah. I'll explain on the way."

"Thanks, Sydney," Charlie told her. "You're welcome to work a shift any time. Might have to get you on the books, you know, to make it legal and all."

"I'll think about it," Sydney replied. "Appreciated!"

"I'll take the apron," I offered. "I could use something familiar at the moment. Never thought I'd crave monotony, but given all this craziness…"

Sydney handed me her pad and apron. Mine were back at the trailer. I could make do.

With a nod, Charlie shuffled back to his office and shut the door firmly. Gareth and Sydney left to do their research. Everyone was off looking for gods. Thankfully, the bar was bare, and the restaurant was mostly empty. Only a few locals enjoying coffee in the corner.

I leaned against the bar next to Grace, who inclined toward me, her red curls dangling in front of inquisitive eyes.

"So, how are things going?" Grace asked, her voice low. "You ran off earlier looking stressed as all get out. Charlie too. Everything okay?"

I sighed, wiping down a section of the bar with a rag. "It's complicated."

"I'll bet." Grace glanced toward Charlie's office. "What's up with you two anyway? He sure lit out of here quick when you called."

I shook my head. "Men are the last thing on my mind right now, trust me."

"Oh really?" Grace raised an eyebrow. "Could've fooled me. That Ken Doll follows you around like a lost puppy. And Charlie, well, that man has it for you something fierce."

"We're friends," I stated firmly. "I've got way too much going on to even think about anything else."

I gave her a small smile before turning back to wipe down the bar. Grace meant well, but she didn't understand. How could she? Ever since remembering my past life as the goddess Isis, it seemed every man I came across was trying to get with me. Charlie, Gareth, even that bastard Balzac. It was getting ridiculous.

Grace must have noticed my brooding expression. "What's eating you, sugar?"

I tossed the rag down with a huff. "All my life, men have barely noticed me. They noticed my ass, that's about it. Never me."

Grace made a sympathetic noise. "Story of my life, hun."

"Now, suddenly, every dude I talk to for more than five minutes thinks he's in love with me." I threw my hands up in exasperation. "I don't get it!"

Grace laughed a throaty chuckle. "Aw, poor you. Must be so hard having all those hot men falling all over themselves for your attention."

I shot her a look. "Oh, shut it, you. It's not as great as it sounds."

Her eyes twinkled with mirth. "In that case, you should take two at once. Could be fun."

I rolled my eyes at her suggestion. "Yeah, no thanks. I'm not interested in juggling multiple men."

She leaned on the bar, eyebrows raised. "Not even slightly tempted by the idea? Come on, live a little!"

"Maybe in some other life, but not this one." I snorted.

Grace sighed dramatically. "You're no fun. I guess you've never been the type to jump right into bed with someone."

"Not really my style." I started wiping down the bar again, hoping she'd drop it.

"You only live once, you know. If I could go back and do it again, I'd make every guy work for it," Grace mused. "I'd have more self-respect, more confidence. I'd tell myself every day that I'm a catch and there ain't no fish in the sea quite like me. No more swooning over the first man who pays me a compliment."

I paused in my cleaning, a wry smile touching my lips. "What if you had multiple lives to get it right?"

Grace blinked. "Huh?"

"Like reincarnation," I clarified. "What if you got to live again and again with all your old memories?"

She threw her head back and laughed. "Well, in that case, I'd hope I come back as a lesbian! I'd have a lot less bullshit to deal with."

I snorted at that. Grace grinned and continued, "Knowing me, if I wasn't a lesbian, I'd probably make all the same dumb mistakes when it came to men."

She leaned on the bar, staring up at the ceiling. "It would take me at least a few lifetimes to figure my shit out. I'd probably have to go through a few hundred divorces before I learned anything."

I smiled and shook my head as I listened. Same old Grace.

"But that's me," she clarified, meeting my eyes again. "You've got a good head on your shoulders, Briar. Just because my love life is a shit show doesn't mean yours needs to be."

I nodded slowly, mulling over her words. Grace always gave good advice, even if her own life was chaotic.

I raised an eyebrow. "So what would you do if you were me and had multiple guys after you?"

Grace's eyes lit up mischievously. "Well, in the old days, they used to make men compete for a princess' hand." She grinned. "I'd make those boys fight for you, Briar. No better sight than a bunch of sweaty men wrestling each other!"

I laughed, unable to help myself. Grace's enthusiasm was infectious.

"Even if one was a total jackass, that's okay," she continued animatedly. "Every good story needs a villain who's after the princess. Gotta have a black knight to make things interesting!"

My shoulders shook with laughter. Only Grace could come up with something so ridiculous yet oddly compelling.

"I'm kidding, I'm kidding," she insisted, noticing my reaction. "Mostly, anyway."

Her expression grew more serious. "In all honesty, if I had to do it over, I wouldn't choose anyone until I was absolutely sure he was right. It's not fair to string multiple guys along when you have feelings for more than one."

I nodded slowly. She had a point there.

"Enough about men," I announced, ready to change the subject. "It's not like I have time for romance anyway. Not with all these dead folks coming back to life lately."

Grace opened her mouth to respond but stopped short, her gaze fixed on the entrance.

"Speak of the devil," she muttered.

I turned to see what had caught her attention, and my blood ran cold.

Jim Bob, Nick, and Donnie Honeycut stood in the doorway, the men who had tried to burn me at the stake. Back from the dead and leering hungrily in my direction.

I froze, staring at the three men I'd hoped never to see again. Jim Bob's beady eyes locked with mine, his thin lips twisting into a sinister grin. Beside him, the hulking Honeycut brothers cracked their knuckles menacingly.

My pulse pounded as I glanced around the empty bar. It was only me and Grace working tonight. We were sorely outnumbered if things turned violent.

Grace leaned close to me. "What should we do?" she whispered nervously.

I inhaled sharply, willing my nerves to steady. "Stay calm," I murmured back. "Let me handle this."

Squaring my shoulders, I strode toward the newly undead trio. Jim Bob's grin widened, clearly anticipating an easy target. Little did he know, I wasn't the same scared girl he'd tried to burn at the stake.

"Well, well," I offered coolly. "Back from the grave, I see. To what do we owe the displeasure?"

Jim Bob chuckled. "Don't play coy with me, witch. I know what you are." He glanced at his cronies. "We got unfinished business, the three of us. And this time, we aim to finish it."

I met his glare unflinchingly. "I wouldn't try anything if I were you," I warned, magic crackling at my fingertips.

Jim Bob's smug expression faltered. The Honeycuts shifted uneasily behind him.

"Now get out," I commanded. "Before I send you right back to the hell you crawled out of."

For a moment, no one moved. Then, with muttered curses, the men turned and slunk away into the night.

I exhaled shakily. Crisis averted, for now. Yet something told me this wasn't over.

Grace slipped behind me and knocked on Charlie's door. If he saw them here, well…

Too late to stop that.

Before I knew it, Charlie was standing face to face with Jim Bob, both men trying to stare the other down.

The customers in the back must've sensed the tension. They left some cash on the table and slipped from the bar. We were customer-less.

Charlie and Jim Bob continued to stare each other down, their eyes locked in a silent battle. I could practically feel the air vibrating.

Finally, Charlie spoke. "I don't know what your business is with Briar, but I suggest you leave now before I call the authorities."

Jim Bob sneered. "You think the police can stop us? We were dead, and now we're not. We're unstoppable."

I narrowed my eyes, feeling the anger boiling inside me. "You may have come back from the dead, but that doesn't make you invincible. It sure as hell doesn't give you the right to harm innocent people."

Jim Bob cackled. "Innocent? You're a witch, Briar. A menace to society. You deserve to be punished for your crimes."

I scoffed. "I've done nothing wrong except exist. You, on the other hand, have tried to kill me twice. Who's the real criminal here?"

"And who are you to call her an abomination, asshole?" Charlie asked. "You're the fucking zombie."

"He has a point," Nick Honeycut added.

"Shut up!" Donnie piped in, elbowing his brother a little too hard in the ribs.

Then, a familiar *ding*. The door swung open, and Balzac sauntered in, clapping his hands. He pantomimed a microphone in his hand. "Let's get ready to rumble!"

Balzac had these bastards under his thrall, and we were in for a fight.

The next thing I knew, Charlie's fist met Jim Bob's jaw.

CHAPTER FOURTEEN

Before I could process what was happening, the Honeycut brothers leaped up to join the brawl. Three against one, surrounding Charlie as he shifted into a grizzly, swiping massive paws.

Balzac cackled like a hyena in the distance.

I grabbed a half-empty pitcher off an uncleared table and smashed it over Donnie's empty head. He barely flinched, shards of glass sticking in his greasy mullet. The Neanderthal turned, beady eyes undressing me as he licked his lips. His meaty paw shot out to grab me.

Oh, hell no! I put everything I had into driving the broken pitcher into his face. Blood and teeth sprayed, but he simply kept coming.

I scrambled back, groping for anything to use as a weapon. Nick lunged for me, tackling me onto the pool table. I writhed and clawed as he pinned me down, fumbling at my top. I kneed him right in the marbles, buying me seconds to grab a pool cue and whack him upside the head.

"Git off me, you nasty pervert!" I hollered. The place was pure chaos, like one of those WWE cage matches on pay-per-view.

Charlie had shifted back into human form, clutching his side where Jim Bob had gotten in a good slash with his bowie knife. But that redneck zombie kept coming, rotten flesh hanging off his bones.

"You can't kill what's already dead!" Jim Bob cackled, taking another swipe at Charlie.

My blood boiled watching the foul creature hurt my friend. I felt a power rising in me, hot as lightning. The next thing I knew, light was pouring from my fingertips, scorching Jim Bob to ashes.

I blinked, stunned at what I'd done. The Honeycut brothers stumbled back, rotten faces wide with shock. I blasted them the same way I did Jim Bob. "Ashes to ashes, motherfuckers."

A slow clap echoed through the bar. Balzac emerged from the shadows, grinning like a possum eating shit.

"That's the Isis I love!" His voice oozed smugness. "I knew you had it in you. Join me, my love. If you don't, there are more dead where they came from. I'll keep sending them after your friends until you're left without a choice."

I trembled, overwhelmed by the raw power still coursing through me. But one look at Charlie's bloodied face steeled my resolve.

"Why don't you slither back to the sewer you crawled from?" I snarled at Balzac. If he wanted a fight, I aimed to give him one. Nobody messed with my friends!

Balzac's grin only widened, like I'd told him some hilarious joke. "Oh, I don't think so."

Before I could react, he lunged forward, plunging his hand into Charlie's chest. Charlie released a choked scream as Balzac yanked out his heart, crushing the pulpy mass in his fist.

"No!" I shrieked, rushing to Charlie's side. His face had gone white, blood bubbling on his lips.

Grace stood frozen, hands clapped over her mouth in horror.

I cradled Charlie's head, sobbing. This was all my fault. If I'd gone with Balzac, maybe he'd still be alive.

Balzac loomed over us, dangling Charlie's shredded heart. "You can save him, Isis. I know you can. Bring him back. You are the mistress of death!"

I trembled, tears blurring my vision. The empty cavity in Charlie's chest taunted me. I had the power to fix this, to undo Balzac's evil. But at what cost? Messing with life and death was dangerous business. What if Charlie came back…wrong? Like the others.

Still, looking at his lifeless body, I knew I had to try. I couldn't lose him! Gripping Charlie tight, I summoned the energy from deep within, focusing it into his wound. His back arched, then collapsed. For a terrible moment, nothing happened.

Then his chest hitched, heart beating beneath my palm. Charlie's eyes flew open, and he gasped like a drowning man breaking the surface.

Balzac's slow clap turned my stomach. I stared at him with eyes that could literally kill if I used my power. Would it work against him, though?

Before I could find out, Balzac snapped his fingers and disappeared in a cloud of smoke.

"Fuck!" I shouted. "That bastard."

I held Charlie close to me. He coughed, clutching his chest. "Briar? What…what did you do?"

I smoothed his hair back. "I brought you back. I couldn't let you die!"

He sat up slowly, flexing his fingers. "You shouldn't have. Who knows what I'll become now?" His face clouded with worry.

I shook my head firmly. "I won't let anything happen to you. I swear it."

Then, without thinking, I kissed him. Big mistake—I knew it. But my emotions overwhelmed me.

Charlie pushed me back. "Briar, I want this. God damn it, I've wanted this for so long. Not like this, though."

What could I say? "I'm sorry."

He stared hard at me as if trying to see into my soul. "You have no idea how sorry I am."

With that, he ran out the door.

I sat there on the grimy bar floor, feeling alone and confused. I had brought someone back from the dead, someone who was in love with me, and in a moment of weakness, I'd led him on. Now he'd run off to the gods knew where. I guessed that meant I should have known where he was going, but I didn't. Away from here. Away from me. Most likely scared he'd turn murderous and hurt me or Grace.

Grace tentatively put a hand on my shoulder. "Are you okay?" she asked softly.

I shook my head. "No, I'm not. I don't know what's happening."

Grace's hand tightened on my shoulder, trying to comfort me. "What do we do now?" she asked.

I breathed in deeply, trying to push away the guilt and confusion. "We find Balzac. And we make him pay for what he's done."

Grace nodded with determination in her eyes. "Whatever it takes."

I stood, feeling the strength of my power once again. If Balzac wanted a fight, I would give him one. "First, we need to find Charlie. Coming back like that, well, he probably isn't right."

"You mean he's going to start killing people?" Grace asked.

I sighed. "You know about that?"

Grace brushed a blonde strand of hair from my face. "Honey, I'm the eyes and ears of this place. I hear everything."

I nodded. "Close the bar. I need to reach out to Gareth and Sydney. Balzac is probably going after them next, and I have to get to Charlie before he snaps."

"Give me his number," Grace returned. "I'll warn Gareth. Go get Charlie. He needs you, hun."

CHAPTER FIFTEEN

I shoved through the underbrush with thorns and branches tearing at my arms. "Where are you?" I shouted, my voice echoing through the forest. A flock of spirit crows burst from the trees, cawing angrily at the interruption. I glanced up, watching their translucent forms disappear over the treetops.

"Please, help me find him," I called, softer this time.

A rustle sounded to my left. I turned to see a deer regarding me silently, its dark eyes solemn. It dipped its head once before bounding off into the woods. I scrambled after it, nearly twisting my ankle on roots and stones.

We didn't follow the beaten path I usually took, but I knew where the spirit was leading me. We were headed toward Dorian's sanctuary.

The trees thinned ahead, and I stumbled into the clearing, breathing hard.

Charlie was there, curled up inside the stone circle. A sickly green light writhed around him as his body morphed and changed. One moment, he was a wolf, then a bear, then some strange creature I couldn't name. He howled and growled, clearly in agony.

"Charlie!" I cried, starting forward. The green magic flared, forcing me back a step. I reached for my own power, calling on Isis, but the spirit energy surrounding the circle lashed out. No way I was getting through that. Not even as a goddess.

Charlie's form settled into something almost human, though antlers still sprouted from his head. He began chanting in a language I didn't know, his voice guttural. The foreign words sent a chill down my spine.

I drew a bracing breath. He was still a druid. Was his warped undead mind forcing him to do something abominable? "Hang on, Charlie," I whispered. "I'm gonna get you out of this, I swear."

Somehow, some way, I'd find a way to save him. I had to believe that.

I paced the edge of the circle, racking my brain for something, anything I could do to help Charlie. His chanting grew louder, more insistent, the foreign words echoing through the trees. I caught a name repeated over and over. *Morrigan.*

Charlie's form settled into human once more, though the antlers remained. He threw back his head, arms outstretched.

"Morrigan!" he cried. "I offer myself as your vessel! Take me, use me as you will!"

My breath caught in my throat. What was happening to him?

"Charlie, no!" I shouted. "Fight this! You have to fight!"

He collapsed to his knees, body wracked with spasms as he transformed again. Fur sprouted along his skin as he cried out in agony. I had to look away, tears burning my eyes.

When I turned back, Charlie was human again, panting hard. He'd shed his fur as quickly as he'd grown it. His eyes found mine, and I saw a flash of the man I knew.

"Briar," he choked out. "I love you…always have. I'm sorry. Before I changed and lost myself, I did what I had to—"

Then his expression changed, going cold and blank. He tilted his head, regarding me curiously. When he spoke again, his voice was different. Still Charlie's, but the tone was all wrong.

"You meddle in affairs beyond your understanding, Isis."

I stumbled back, stunned. Whatever was speaking through Charlie, it wasn't him. Not anymore.

I swallowed hard. "Who are you?"

Charlie's mouth curved into a smirk. He straightened to his full height, looming over me.

"I am the Morrigan," he declared, spreading his arms wide. "Phantom queen and mistress of death."

My blood turned to ice in my veins. I only knew a few things about her. A dangerous Celtic goddess, a harbinger of war and strife. She was one of the deities Charlie suggested might have the power to help with our situation, but this was something else. He'd let this strange goddess take over his body. What the hell had Charlie gotten himself into?

"What do you want?" I demanded with fists clenched.

Charlie—no, the Morrigan—chuckled. "Your druid tells me you require my aid. I must admit, it amuses me that a prideful goddess like you might need me to save you. I can do what he asks, but it will come with a price, Isis."

I bristled at the goddess' name. "Don't call me that. My name is Briar."

"As you wish." The Morrigan inclined Charlie's head. "If you want my help, you must relinquish your power to me."

My power? Did she mean my magic as Isis? Or the rest of it? The powers I'd always had? I'd tried to reject that part of myself for so long, but now the fate of the world might depend on it. Could I really trust this goddess who called herself a phantom queen? As I searched my past life's memories, I found little about this strange deity. Perhaps she was right. The Egyptian gods didn't play well with others.

"If I give up my power, you'll repair the veil between worlds?" I asked slowly. "You'll stop the end times?"

The Morrigan smiled, sending a chill down my spine. "I will do what I can, but Set must be dealt with first. If we heal the veil now, he would simply tear it open again. As could you, which is why you must give me your power. I will not suffer you to ruin the world a second time."

I grunted. "Look, I didn't know what I was doing. I do now."

"Be that as it may, such errors come with consequences. If you wish me to help you, I must claim your power."

I huffed. "Fine. Then take it! Fix all this shit!"

The Morrigan laughed. "Not yet. No, it isn't time. First, you must defeat your brother."

"I have to kill Set?"

The Morrigan nodded. "He will not be easily thwarted, even by the likes of me. It will require both of us to bind him and send him back to the otherworld."

I snatched a breath. This wasn't only about me anymore. If surrendering my magic could fix things, it was a small price to pay.

"Okay," I told her. "You've got a deal."

The Morrigan laughed, a sound both musical and sinister. "Very well. We will stop Set together. We will need others. Those who wield your strange people's magic."

I nodded. "I have friends. They'll help."

The Morrigan rolled Charlie's eyes. "Friends. You have *friends* but call yourself a goddess?"

I snorted. "Would you prefer I call them my subjects?"

"Not at all, dear. I simply find your…humility amusing. You've changed."

I nodded. "Yeah, well, this Isis shit is like old memories buried in my mind. I don't feel like a goddess. Just a girl, a waitress, trying to save the world."

The Morrigan tilted her head, regarding me with those ancient, inhuman eyes. Charlie's warm brown irises were now an icy blue that pierced my soul.

"You have a certain fire about you," she remarked. "I can see why my vessel is drawn to you."

I resisted the urge to shudder. "What do you mean, drawn to me?"

The Morrigan grinned. "Oh, my dear, do not play coy. The druid has been enamored with you for some time now. He seeks your approval, your attention, your affection. It is endearing."

My heart sank. "Charlie. He said he loved me."

The Morrigan shrugged, Charlie's body moving awkwardly with the gesture. "He does. That does not mean you must love him in return. It does not mean you must return his feelings. Love is a fickle thing, Briar. It comes and goes like the tide. Take it from me. I loved a mortal once. I paid the price for it."

I swallowed hard, trying to keep my emotions in check. "What happened?"

The Morrigan's expression darkened. "He rejected me. He chose another woman over me, and I lost control. I killed him and those he loved. I destroyed everything." She shook her head, regret crossing her features. "This is what happens to the Divine who set their hearts on mortals. It never ends well."

I frowned. "What are you saying? That I can't love anyone?"

The Morrigan shrugged. "I am saying love can be a dangerous thing. It can cloud your judgment and make you vulnerable. In times like these, you need to be strong, detached. If you are not, Set will treat your love as a weakness. He'll use it against you."

I gritted my teeth. "He's threatened to kill my friends and raise them into his army if I don't join him."

The Morrigan's eyes hardened. "He is not beyond such cruelty, but you cannot allow him to have that power over you. You must be willing to sacrifice your loved ones, if necessary, for the greater good."

I shook my head in disbelief. "I can't do that. I won't do that."

The Morrigan's voice grew cold. "Then you are not fit to be a goddess. This is the reality of our existence. We are not human. We are not mortal. We are beings of power, of magic, of strength. The fate of the world rests on your shoulders, Briar. You must be willing to make sacrifices and do what is necessary. Even if it means giving up everything you hold dear."

I inhaled deeply, feeling the weight of her words. "Well, if you take my power, none of that will matter. I'll be human again anyway."

The Morrigan laughed. "I cannot make you a mortal, even if I take your power. What I require is your control over the dead. Your ability to resurrect souls. That, my dear, you've proven unfit to wield. You've destroyed the balance and cast your magic without knowledge of the damage it could cause."

I shook my head. "I was trying to make things right."

"People die," the Morrigan commented. "This is the natural order."

I shook my head. "You don't understand. A warlock used dark magic to save my life. It turned him into a killer. I owed it to him. And those people died before their time."

The Morrigan tilted her head—Charlie's head. "Who are you to know if it was their time?"

I shrugged. "Well, come to find out, I am a goddess."

"That doesn't mean you have the right to decide when it's someone's time. If someone dies, no matter the means, it is their time. Even this body, this vessel. It was his time."

"No, it wasn't! Fucking Set killed him!"

The Morrigan's eyes flared with rage. "Are you not listening to a word I speak? You Egyptians. You think you know better than the rest of us. It's infuriating."

I shook my head. "I barely know who I even am. My life as Isis before is more like a movie in my mind than a memory."

The Morrigan sighed and softened her gaze. "I understand your frustration, Briar. You must try to remember who you were and what you stood for. Your error was not on account of your divinity but your humanity."

"So I fucked up because I'm human?"

The Morrigan signed. "For all her faults, Isis was a goddess of balance, of healing, of magic. She would never have cast a spell without understanding its consequences. She would have known that death is a natural part of life and that resurrecting souls unnaturally could upset the delicate balance of the universe."

"But I—Isis. She resurrected Osiris."

"A god! Not a mortal! And she knew how to repair the veil when she was done. You did not!"

I nodded, feeling guilty for my ignorance. "You're right. I need to learn how to control my powers, to use them responsibly."

The Morrigan smiled. "It doesn't matter. Our agreement remains. I will claim this power so that you do not repeat your error. First, we must deal with Set. He is a threat to the balance of all worlds."

"I'll do whatever it takes," I promised.

"Good," the Morrigan replied. "Because we have much to do."

CHAPTER SIXTEEN

The Morrigan's cold, bony fingers gripped my wrist, her nails digging in. I winced. For a goddess, she had the claws of a harpy.

"Take me to where you last saw Set," she rasped, her voice like nails on a chalkboard. Charlie's usually warm brown eyes were now flat and black, filled with an ancient, calculating darkness. "I can sense his magic. Track him."

I yanked my arm back. "So what, you sniff him out like a dog?"

The Morrigan released a cackling laugh, sending chills up my spine. "Given this host's proclivity for the canine form, an apt comparison."

"Right." I shivered, glancing back through the trees toward Dorian's sanctuary.

"The bar, then," I told her. "That's where I last saw the sonofabitch, right after he yanked Charlie's heart from his chest."

The Morrigan grinned, baring Charlie's straight white teeth. "Lead the way."

I turned and trudged down the leaf-strewn path away from Dorian's sanctuary, listening to the Morrigan's shuffling steps behind me. My spirit companions lurked in the distance, watching from afar as we two goddesses marched through the woods toward our destination.

When we arrived at Charlie's, the place was trashed. Chairs overturned, glass shattered across the floor, tables smashed. All the result of our fight with Jim Bob and the Honeycuts.

Gareth and Sydney were already there, surveying the damage. Sydney gasped when she saw us.

"What the hell happened?" Gareth asked, eyebrows raised.

"Balzac happened," I told him. "He came back with Jim Bob and those Honeycut assholes. Resurrected and looking to party."

Sydney's face reddened. "Those monsters tried to burn you and Dorian at the stake!"

I waved my hand. "Yeah, well, they're ash again now. Thanks to yours truly. Balzac's still out there somewhere, though."

Gareth was staring at Charlie, or rather, the Morrigan inside Charlie, with a curious expression.

"Gareth, Sydney. Meet the Morrigan," I announced. "She's, uh…borrowing Charlie's body for now. After Balzac killed Charlie, I resurrected him—"

"You did what?" Gareth's eyes widened.

"Look, I know it was reckless. Charlie wasn't happy about it either. He invoked the Morrigan and asked her to take his body before he lost control and turned homicidal like the other resurrected."

Sydney blinked in surprise. Gareth only nodded thoughtfully.

"A wise choice on Charlie's part," he stated. "We need the power of the goddess to heal the veil and defeat Set."

"Yeah, eventually the Morrigan will help us with that spell. First, we gotta take care of Balzac." I gestured to the goddess. "According to her, we need to defeat Set and send him back through the veil before we can repair it."

The Morrigan smiled, an unsettling expression on Charlie's normally kind face. "You and Gareth are two of the most powerful witches here. If you can keep Set occupied, Briar and I will be able to force him back through the veil."

"What do you need from us?" Gareth asked.

The Morrigan leaned forward, steepling Charlie's fingers in a gesture that looked bizarrely out of place on him.

"Here is what we must do," she explained. "Gareth, Sydney, you will engage Set directly, drawing him into battle. Focus your attacks on his physical form and keep him occupied with your magic. Briar and I will use that opportunity to move in unseen and bind him."

She withdrew a slender cord from Charlie's jacket pocket. It glimmered with a strange light, clearly enchanted in some way.

"After we have him bound, I will open the portal and force Set back through the veil into the realm of the gods where he belongs. With the added power of Isis, the binding should be strong enough to contain him."

I studied the cord anxiously. So much depended on that little loop of rope. Did Charlie have it all along, or was it a common rope the Morrigan had repurposed? I didn't know. It didn't matter. The plan was sound but dangerous.

Gareth cracked his knuckles, eyes hard with determination. "Sounds good. Let's do this."

Sydney squared her shoulders and gave a curt nod. She looked nervous but resolute.

I drew a deep breath. "Okay. Let's end this, once and for all."

The Morrigan raised Charlie's finger. "One moment. Set's magic lingers here. I can follow it."

She closed her eyes, and a moment later, a strange expression flickered across her face. "Ah. I believe I have found it." She opened her eyes, looking at Gareth. "Would you kindly open the door?"

Gareth stepped forward, a sense of trepidation in his move-ments. He grabbed the door handle, pushing it open with a creak.

The Morrigan smiled. "Follow me. Try to keep up."

Then, she shifted into the form of a raven. Whether she did it with her own power or Charlie's, I wasn't sure.

She flew out the door, and we followed. The Morrigan perched on the branch of a tree and cawed at us.

"I guess we follow." I shrugged.

Gareth shook his head. "This is going to be interesting."

I nodded. "And dangerous. Look, you two. If you don't want to—"

"Stop," Sydney insisted. "We're with you."

Gareth nodded in agreement. "This ends tonight. But Briar, are you sure you can trust this Morrigan?"

I shook my head. "Not at all, but we need her. From what she's told me, she's concerned with restoring the balance."

As we followed the Morrigan's lead, I couldn't help but feel a creeping sense of dread. This was it. The final showdown. The fate of the world rested on our shoulders. My mind raced with the possibilities of what could go wrong, but I pushed those thoughts aside. I had to focus.

We came upon an abandoned warehouse on the outskirts of town. Old, rusted boats littered the lot. The Morrigan landed on one of them, then returned to Charlie's form.

"Set is inside." She pointed to a door. "Be careful. He's not alone."

"Not alone?" I asked. "What do you mean?"

The Morrigan sniffed at the air. "I'd say he's gathered a small army. Fifteen, maybe twenty, resurrected dead accompany him. This will not be an easy task."

Gareth shook his head. "I'm calling the Morai. Those undead bastards are invulnerable to our magic, but if all you need is a distraction, we can do it."

No sooner did Gareth get on his phone than a large swirl of magic swelled over the warehouse. It spun into a tornado that shot out into splinters of magic as far as the eye could see.

Gareth lowered his phone from his ear. "What the hell?"

"He's resurrected the dead," the Morrigan revealed.

I gulped. "How many?"

The Morrigan shook Charlie's head. "All of them. We must hurry. More will arrive here soon. We do not have time to wait for your friends. If Set gathers them and takes control, he'll be impossible to reach."

CHAPTER SEVENTEEN

We couldn't wait for Morai reinforcements, but that didn't mean we had to take on the crowd alone. The Morrigan wanted a distraction? I could give her one.

I thrust my hands toward the sky with my fingers spread like a preacher at Sunday service. I reached out to every spirit all around. With my power stronger than ever, I could connect to thousands. Maybe millions if you included the dead insects.

Balzac might have had all of the world's dead. Did he really raise all of them, like everyone who'd died in all of human history? Maybe. Still, he couldn't gather all of them at once. They couldn't teleport. For the moment, there were more dead animal spirits in the area than humans.

The woods trembled, leaves shaking free from branches. Squirrels and raccoons poked out from tree hollows. Deer raised their heads, ears pricked. With my Isis power, I gave them physical form. Before, I needed a special totem. Now, I only needed a thought.

A chorus of howls and screeches rang out as animals poured from the forest, their forms wavering like smoke. Raccoons and squirrels scampered at my feet. My black bear, Smokey, lumbered forward, followed by a pack of wolves with moon-bright eyes led by Roy. Owls and hawks circled overhead while snakes slithered through the grass. I had never connected to snakes before. It was probably a mental block because, well, ew. Now, I had no hesitation.

The sensation was exhilarating as the power thrummed in my veins. I loosed a wild laugh like I was being mercilessly tickled. I couldn't help it. "All right, everyone!" I shouted to the animals as much as my friends. "Let's go kick some undead ass!"

I whooped and thrust my fist up. The animals charged, a tsunami of fur, feathers, and fangs. As they flowed around me, I laughed, drunk on primal energy.

Take that, Balzac! You mess with this Ozark witch, you get the claws!

Gareth strode up beside me, hands glowing with magic. With a flourish, he traced a symbol in the air. The lines blazed crimson before shooting toward the warehouse in a concussive blast.

The wall exploded in a shower of brick and mortar. My army of spirits flooded through the gaping hole.

A raven alighted on my shoulder. "Nice work, Isis," the Morrigan remarked, a smile in her voice.

I rolled my eyes. "It's Briar."

"Of course." She rubbed her beak against my cheek affectionately before launching herself through the breached wall, melding into the tide of animals.

Sydney fell in on my other side, face set with determination. The three of us shared a nod before charging into the warehouse on the heels of my spirit army.

Gareth and I slung spells as we ran, sending the undead flying like bowling pins. My magic felt wild, primal—no longer the careful, cautious magic I'd clung to these last few years. Each blast erupted from me with the force of a geyser. I whooped again, drunk on power.

We plowed through the warehouse, spirits snarling and snapping on all sides. The undead were distracted and confused. Perfect. Now, to find Balzac and end this nightmare.

I spotted him across the warehouse, lounging on a makeshift throne of crates. He sat with one leg crossed casually over the other, regarding the chaos with an amused smile. When he saw me coming, his grin spread wider. He leaned forward, steepling his fingers.

"Well, well. If it isn't the goddess herself, come to grace me with her presence." He clapped his hands together. "That's the Isis I know and love! Come on, doll, let's have some fun."

My lip curled in a snarl, magic flaring brighter around my hands. I started toward him, ready to blast that smug look off his face.

Before I got close, a blur of black feathers shot past me. The Morrigan, still in raven form, dove directly for Balzac. At the last second, she shapeshifted, becoming Charlie again. With practiced ease, she looped her enchanted rope around Balzac, binding his arms to his sides.

He roared in rage, writhing against the rope. The Morrigan only laughed and gave the cord a sharp tug.

"It's over, Set," she pronounced. "You've caused enough trouble here."

Balzac giggled. "You're too late. The chaos has already begun!"

With a flourish of Charlie's free hand, the Morrigan opened a portal, its horizon like a black, simmering abyss.

The Morrigan dragged Balzac toward it. He struggled furiously, but her rope held fast.

"You can't stop this!" he shouted. "You're too late! You need me, Isis! You can't end this without me!"

"We'll see about that." I stepped toward him, magic tingling at my fingertips. With a mighty heave, I launched him through the portal.

Before it closed, a tide of undead poured into the warehouse.

Snarling and clawing, they hurled themselves through the gateway en masse. I watched in horror as the surging horde swept the Morrigan away into the portal.

"No! Charlie!" I screamed.

I sprinted for the portal, desperate to follow her through. Gareth grabbed me around the waist, yanking me back at the last second.

"Let me go!" I shrieked, straining against him. "I have to save Charlie, and we need her! We can't stop this without the Morrigan!"

"It's too late!" He dragged me away, my feet scrabbling for purchase. Then, the inky portal shrank into nothing.

"Damn it!" I screamed.

"The portal's closed." Gareth's voice was too damn calm, given the situation. "We need to get out of here!"

I collapsed against him, the fight draining from me. Sobs wracked my body. Without the Morrigan, we didn't stand a chance.

We were screwed. Sideways, backward, every which way. Seven days a week, royally fucked.

Sydney grabbed my shoulder, giving me a shake. "Hey, I hate to interrupt." She nodded toward the warehouse entrance. "We've got more company."

I lifted my head to see dozens more of the resurrected dead staggering inside. Their enraged shouts echoed off the concrete walls as they dove toward us, not like zombies in the movies but like healthy men and women high on rage and energy drinks.

They surrounded us. I blasted a few of them to ash, but I didn't know if I could target all of them at once. We didn't have time for me to sit and think about it while I consulted past-life memories.

Gareth's jaw clenched. "We have to leave."

He clasped Sydney's hand, then mine. I barely had time to take a breath before he teleported us out of the warehouse.

We reappeared atop a cliff overlooking the building. Below, the parking lot flooded with undead. They poured from every direction, converging on the warehouse like rivers merging into one.

Hundreds upon hundreds shuffled through the darkness. Maybe thousands. I'd never seen so many in one place.

It was like Woodstock for the dead. Minus all the peace and love.

My heart dropped into my stomach. There had to be something I could use, something to remember in my arsenal of past-life magic. I knew I could turn a few to ash at a time, but how could I stop an army of this size? And by size, I was talking every man, woman, and child who'd ever perished, all making their way here to the Ozarks.

This was what the Book of the Dead foretold. The dead would rule the world. Not with kings or queens but with chaos.

Gareth's voice was grim. "With or without the Morrigan, we have to find a way."

I swallowed hard. He was right. As the only remaining goddess, it was up to me now. What could I do, though? I needed another god or goddess to repair the veil. Even that was pointless if all the dead were already here. Somehow, I had to find a way to end all this at once. A way to suck the life—if you could call it that—out of each one on a global scale.

As I racked my mind, I couldn't find an answer. Nothing in my own memory, for sure, but every corner of my mind belonging to ancient Isis turned up more dead ends.

I shook my head. "There's nothing we can do. It's done. All we can do now is hope we survive and help others do the same."

"Aiden." Sydney shook her head. "We need to get to him. To save him. We can take him with us to the Morai HQ. These dead bastards don't have a god to lead them anymore."

"Brilliant." Gareth nodded. "The whole place is shrouded from view. The resurrected won't find us there. At the least, it gives us a place to hide while we come up with a plan."

I nodded. "Yeah, but first, we go get my brother. My guess, since Sydney is with us, he's back at the trailer."

CHAPTER EIGHTEEN

We landed with a thud in the crabgrass. The familiar sight of my beat-up singlewide greeted me, along with the stench of death and decay. Sitting on the steps was Aiden, shotgun in hand, surrounded by a pile of zombie corpses with their heads blown clean off.

"Well, I'll be damned." Sydney scrunched her nose at the carnage. "I thought pink flamingos and old appliances gave a place redneck curb appeal. Headless corpses take it to a whole new level."

Aiden jumped up, beaming with pride. "Hey, y'all! Wait 'til I tell ya how I figured out blasting their noggins off keeps 'em down for good. Tried bullets first, but that only made 'em mad as a stepped-on copperhead. So I got to thinking." He tapped his temple, grinning. "Can't bite if they ain't got no teeth to chomp with! A little buckshot to the brainpan blows those suckers away for good."

I sighed, the grisly scene sinking my heart even lower. We'd failed, letting Set escape. Now the dead walked, Dorian was still absent, and Charlie was dead. Again. As Aiden prattled on about his zombie-slaying brilliance, I tuned him out, grief and fear rising in my throat like bile. We needed a miracle, or we were all damned.

I cut Aiden off mid-sentence. "Charlie's dead. For real this time."

Aiden's face fell, his exuberance vanishing. "Aw, hell, not again. What happened?"

"Doesn't matter now. We need to get to the coven house where it's safe." I tried to keep my voice steady, but inside I was screaming. Charlie, my dear friend, was gone. Possibly for good this time if I couldn't figure out how to bring him back.

Aiden shuddered. "That weird old place gives me the heebie-jeebies."

I put my hand on his shoulder. "I know, but we've got no other choice. Grab your things. We need to go."

He nodded, ducking inside the trailer. I stood there, heart cracking in two. What hope did we have? I had no answers. Only the lingering taste of failure and the cold whisper of fear in my gut. Disaster wasn't coming. It was already here. There was no way to stop that many enraged dead people who were, pardon the pun, dead set on sowing chaos everywhere they went.

We arrived at Morai HQ, the coven's stately old Victorian mansion, in seconds. Gareth teleported us directly into the grand foyer with its polished oak floor and crystal chandelier. Normally, the place filled me with a sense of power and purpose. Now, it felt empty.

Aiden whistled, impressed as always by Gareth's abilities. "Man, I wish I could do that! Beats the hell out of my rusty old truck."

I managed a weak smile. "Why don't you poke around the library and see if you can help the others research this mess?"

His eyes widened in mock astonishment. "Me? In a library? Do your books have pictures?"

Sydney scratched her head. "Actually, more than you'd think. Come on, I'll show you."

I sighed, wishing I shared Aiden's ability to find pleasure even in the bleakest situation. The weight pressing down on me was too heavy for laughter.

My feet carried me down the shadowed hallway toward the ritual room, almost against my will. I pushed open the heavy oak door and slipped inside, closing it firmly behind me.

The room was cold and silent, the sacred tools and magical implements shrouded in darkness. I sank to my knees on the stone floor, tears finally spilling down my cheeks.

"Oh, Charlie," I whispered. "I don't know if I can save you this time. I've failed you…failed everyone."

I bowed my head, hugging my arms around myself. I didn't know if I could resurrect Charlie again. Not without a body to work with. Besides, he was twice-baked dead. Made for great potatoes. Not so much when it came to corpses. He was gone. At least he took a god and a goddess with him. Maybe the Morrigan's presence would ensure he found peace in the afterlife.

Never had I felt so lost and afraid, not even as long as I could remember in my first life as Isis. What good were my powers now? I didn't feel like a goddess. Not even like a powerful witch. Only a frightened young woman whose magic didn't seem strong enough to do the job. Certainly not enough to unravel an apocalypse that was already in motion.

I didn't know how long I knelt there in the dark before anger rose in me, hot and fierce. I stood abruptly, fists clenched.

"No. I won't give up." My voice echoed off the chamber walls. "Whatever it takes, I'll find a way to fix this."

I strode from the ritual room, determination burning away my doubts. Most people, when faced with adversity, refuse to get their hopes up for fear of disappointment. I didn't know if that was wise, though. Why be bummed out, pessimistic, and unhappy all the time if what you fear is that you're going to be unhappy when you're disappointed? Might as well hope for the best, even in a shit storm, rather than wallow in worst-case or even likely apocalyptic scenarios.

Maybe all would go to crap, but I'd feel sorry for myself then. Until then, against all odds, I had to believe we'd find a way to beat this thing. I was Isis reborn. Failure was not an option.

I marched down the hallway, my sneakers squeaking on the hardwood. As I turned the corner, I nearly collided with Aiden.

"Whoa there, firecracker." He grasped my arms to steady me. "Where you off to in such a hurry?"

I shook free of his hold. "The library. I was coming to join you. I need answers."

Aiden fell into step beside me. "Well, you're in luck 'cause answers are my middle name." At my skeptical look, he amended, "Okay, my middle name is actually Eugene, but that's not important right now."

Despite everything, I felt my lips quirk. There was something calming about Aiden's ignorant optimism. Better to be him than an educated stick-in-the-mud.

"Any luck researching?" I asked as we entered the library's grand foyer.

"Not yet." Aiden scratched his head, eyeing the rows of ancient tomes. "But me and books, we don't really get along, if you know what I mean."

I scanned the shelves, fingers trailing over dusty spines until I found the text I sought. A heavy, leather-bound tome marked with hieroglyphs.

"This may help," I murmured, cracking it open on a table. Aiden peered over my shoulder as I turned the fragile pages.

"Can you read that chicken scratch?"

I nodded, though I was surprised I could. Another benefit of my past life. My head throbbed as I dove in. It was a bunch of bullshit about grain stores, weather patterns, and other economics of ancient Cairo. Nothing remotely magical. I slammed the book shut in frustration.

"It's no use. I can't focus." I dragged my hands down my face. "My mind is too chaotic, and there are too many books here."

Aiden's hand settled on my shoulder. "Hey, don't sweat it. We've hit walls before and busted right through 'em. This zombie apocalypse don't stand a chance against us."

Despite everything, his optimism sparked my own. This was much bigger than anything we'd ever faced, but if Aiden could stay positive, why couldn't I? I offered a small smile.

"You're right. I can't give up yet. There must be something in these books to help reverse all this."

I selected another text, this one on necromancy and reviving the dead. Exactly the opposite of what we wanted to do at the moment. At least I was in the right ballpark, and maybe there'd be something about how to undo a resurrection or seal a veil in a way I didn't immediately know. Even if the book didn't have the answers, perhaps it would spark an ancient memory that held the answer.

Hope kindled within me once more as Aiden and I got to work researching. With my friends by my side, I would find a way to set things right.

CHAPTER NINETEEN

The glare of the big screen TV in the Morai sitting room, complete with wet bar, burned my eyes as I flipped through channels. News helicopter footage showed zombies shambling through city streets, tearing people limb from limb. On another channel, some preacher shouted, "Judgment Day is here! Will you be a sheep or a goat?"

"Well, shit on a shingle," I muttered. "This is really baaaaaad."

Aiden's laughter made me jump. I hadn't heard him come in.

"Sheep joke!" he crowed. "Good one, Briar."

"Look, the preacher said if I'm a sheep, I'll get saved. Not so with the goats."

Aiden shook his head. "Don't think it matters much. Sheep and goats are all gonna get fucked. Which I realize sounds really weird, but that's not what I meant. I swear."

I chuckled. "I believe you, Aiden."

"Thing is, we don't need sheep and goats. We need lions, tigers, and bears!"

"Oh my!" I chuckled.

"Damn straight," Aiden agreed. "Thankfully, you can call a few of those up. Maybe start a war between dead animals and dead people."

I shook my head. "Honestly, I don't know if it will matter. The whole plan before was to deal with Set, then fix the veil so no one could tear it open again. And so the dead we killed wouldn't find their way back as soon as we dropped them.

"It's so horrible, I can't help but laugh," I added. "Gallows humor, defense mechanism, whatever you want to call it."

Aiden shrugged and shuffled over. "Could be worse. Least we got cold beer and good company for the end times."

"Amen to that." I clinked my bottle against his.

We drank in silence for a minute, contemplating the madness unfolding on the TV screen. Riots, zombies, biblical prophecies of the dead rising. Then, for some reason, soap operas. I mean, the world was ending. Did it really matter who slept with who, or who was at fault, or whatever shit soap operas are about?

Then again, every other station was broadcasting the news. Some people needed a little escape. Given my choices, though, I'd probably rather face a billion zombies than sit through a single episode of *General Hospital*. Just saying.

Clearly, this wasn't an Ozark problem. It was worldwide now.

"Reckon we oughta ride it out here 'til this all blows over?" Aiden asked.

I nodded. "Good a plan as any. At the least, we'll go out in a blaze of glory."

We chuckled grimly and turned our attention back to the TV, waiting to see what fresh hell would rise next.

I shook my head, trying to clear the dark thoughts. Aiden's optimism was infectious.

"It's better to laugh than worry, right?" he suggested.

I nodded. "True. Not like fretting will help the situation."

"Exactly!" Aiden leaned on the bar top, beer in hand. "When I'm upset, it's hard to think past it. When I'm laughing or excited, it's easy to think about other things."

"The power of positive thinking," I stated wryly.

Aiden nodded. "A lot of people say I only think about one thing, but that's not true! I don't only think about titties when I'm excited or happy, but it's always T and A! And if I'm in a really good mood, I'll think about the P, too. So that's three things I can think about at once, minimum."

I laughed, shaking my head. "You're a real sage, Aiden. A genuine mathematician. An intellectual giant."

"I know, right?" He preened comically.

We shared a smile before I sighed and cracked open the book I'd brought in here, the one on necromancy. As I expected, it contained a lot about raising the dead but not much about putting them back in the ground again. Other than by killing them one at a time, which wasn't viable when you were dealing with hordes of millions. Nuke them, maybe, but that would leave the whole world a radioactive wasteland and kill more people who could rise again. I wouldn't put it past the world's governments to try it, though. What they didn't realize was with the veil compromised, anything could rise again at any time.

Maybe even Charlie and the Morrigan. Probably Set, too. But there was no guaranteeing any of that.

I stared blankly at Aiden, processing my thoughts.

"If I knew how to time travel, maybe I could go back and do things differently," I stated finally.

Aiden shook his head. "That won't work. They haven't made the DeLorean since the early eighties. They're hard to find."

I looked at him, dumbfounded. Of all the asinine, absurd things to say. I wanted to break the news that *Back to the Future* was only a movie, but I bit my tongue, refusing to comment. Aiden probably thought the Nazis stole the Ark of the Covenant, too. And that tornadoes could take you to the Land of Oz.

Instead, I turned my focus back to the book. I flipped through the pages, scanning for anything that might explain the madness happening in the world. The answers still eluded me.

Aiden rambled on, oblivious as always. I tuned him out, losing myself in magical theory and arcane history. Every now and then, I picked up enough of what he was talking about to laugh. It was good for me. It kept me grounded. Otherwise, with all this reading, I'd probably start glossing over things out of impatience.

No, the key was here somewhere, buried in these ancient pages. I had to keep digging.

Eventually, I leaned back in my chair, rubbing my eyes. "This is hopeless. There's nothing here that can help us."

Aiden looked over, concern etched on his face. "You've been at it for hours. Maybe it's time to take a break. Get some fresh air."

I sighed. "Yeah, you're probably right. Maybe a walk will clear my head."

We headed outside, the air thick with the stench of decay and death. It was like walking through a graveyard. Except this was the whole world now.

I shuddered, the enormity of the situation settling heavily on my shoulders. I scanned the horizon and reached out to my spirit friends to ensure we weren't in the path of any approaching dead. We were good for the time being. Still, that smell remained on the wind. Clearly, when we'd brought back the recently deceased before, it wasn't as gruesome as raising all the dead.

"One spell did this." I sighed. "Before Set released that magic, the resurrections were more intermittent."

Aiden tilted his head. "Well, if one spell started it, could one spell end it?"

I sighed. "I don't know. It's sort of like trying to put toothpaste back in the tube."

Aiden nodded. "Yeah, what's the point? You squeeze out the tube, and you have two options. Scoop all the toothpaste up, put it in a cup or a little bag, and make the best of it. Or, you say fuck it and buy another tube."

I blinked. "Holy shit."

"What is it?"

"That was brilliant, Aiden!"

Aiden frowned. "It was?"

"Yes!" I clapped my hands. "Isis did this before. I mean, she didn't stop a zombie apocalypse, but she created other realms. Pocket dimensions."

Aiden snorted. "A dimension of pockets? Full of lint and everything?"

"Not that kind of pocket." I shook my head. "The point is, maybe we don't need to put all the dead back in hell, or heaven, or wherever. We don't even need to kill them. Set used his power to call them all to himself. If I can figure out how to do that and create a pocket dimension, a new afterlife, I can try to lure them all inside."

"So what, you hook a brain on a fishing rod and toss it in your little portal?"

I shook my head. "We force Set to relocate."

"Ball Sack is already gone. How are you going to do that?"

I shook my head. "I have a friend there. Charlie is in the same realm he's in. So is the Morrigan. More than that, Osiris is there."

"Osiris?" Aiden echoed.

I nodded. "I remember now. After Set killed him and I brought him back, he returned as a mummy. He wasn't whole. My son, Horus, challenged Set to rule the gods on earth. Osiris went to rule the underworld. We sent Set into the domain of the one god who wants vengeance on him more than any other."

Aiden cleared his throat. "I'm not sure I follow. So what if your past life's hubby gets to torture Set in the underworld? How does that help us now?"

"I need to talk to him. If I can create a pocket dimension, and we can toss Set into it and bind him so he can't escape again, I can open the portal here, on Earth. Wide open to Set's little prison realm. Meanwhile, since the undead were drawn to him already and still seem determined to come where his magic called them, they should head into the portal with him."

Aiden's eyes widened. "So you *are* putting the toothpaste back in the tube."

"No, this is a different tube entirely. Which, I guess, is just as difficult. That doesn't matter, though. This isn't a toothpaste problem. It's an undead problem. Come on. I need to run this idea past Gareth and Sydney."

CHAPTER TWENTY

The smell of burnt coffee smacked me in the nostrils as I walked into the Morai HQ's kitchen. I wrinkled my nose and waved a hand in front of my face.

"Jeez, Gare, you tryin' to wake the dead with that swill?" I asked.

He glanced up from an ancient Mr. Coffee maker, his baby blues twinkling. "Hey, don't knock my brew. This stuff could melt steel."

I snorted. "More like melt your insides."

Sydney breezed in, her long dark braid swinging behind her. "Ooh, is that coffee I smell?"

I shot her an incredulous look. "You call that stench coffee?"

"It's not that bad." She made a beeline for the pot.

I rolled my eyes. These Ozark witches had no taste.

After clearing my throat, I got down to business. "So here's the deal, guys. I gotta hightail it down to the underworld and have a chat with Osiris."

Gareth frowned, arms crossed over his broad chest. "The underworld? You sure that's smart? Isn't that where we sent Set?"

"I know, I know, but Big O's the honcho down there. I'm

remembering more about my past. After I brought him back, he wasn't quite right. Fish in the Nile ate his penis before I could put him back together." I snickered. "Big O couldn't give me the Big O anymore."

"Aw, you poor girl!" Sydney shook her head. "That must've been awful."

Aiden stared at us blankly. "Osiris lost his penis, and you're worried that Briar—I mean, Isis—couldn't get on the stick anymore?"

Sydney shrugged. "A goddess has her needs."

"You're talking about my sister! Plus, that guy lost his dick. That's awful! Like I'd be lost without mine. It always points me where I need to go."

Sydney laughed. "That's not entirely untrue."

I raised my hand to refocus the conversation and bring everyone back in. "According to custom, without a penis, he couldn't rule either. Yeah, the patriarchy shit was pretty thick among the gods in those days."

Gareth nodded. "That's right. So, he went to rule the underworld. I came across that myth in the library. Hard to know how much of these are true, but I take it this one is?"

"Absolutely." I nodded with confidence. "If I can convince Osiris to help, we can whip up a trap dimension, toss Set inside as bait, and make sure he's bound so he can't get out. If we open a door to it from Earth, it'll attract the dead like shit draws in flies."

Sydney perked up. "A pocket dimension? That's genius!"

"I have my moments," I intoned with a smirk.

Gareth stroked his stubbled chin. "How are you gonna open a portal without the Morrigan?"

"Way ahead of ya. I'll rip back open the veil where it already tore. Like pickin' a scab." I made a tearing motion with my hands. "I was once one of the most powerful gods anywhere, but not every god can open portals directly to the underworld, regardless of power. The Morrigan could because within her family, you know, her pantheon, she's the death goddess. I don't have a key. But where a door's been opened already…well, I can kick through it."

Sydney perked up from her notebook, where she'd been jotting down spell ideas. "Open the portal back at the warehouse? That place must be crawling with undead. It was overrun when we left. "

I nodded. "Already thought about that. What if we use Dorian's sanctuary? We only need to channel my spell, the one I use to kill those bastards. It should hold them off or turn them to ash if they dare cross the circle."

Gareth tilted his head. "Yeah, well, one obvious problem with that. Dorian's sanctuary is probably ten miles away. We could try to erect a new stone circle around the warehouse, but setting stones like that isn't easy, even with magic. Plus, we'd have the same problem. We'd have to do it while fighting off the undead."

I pinched my chin. "Charlie said something interesting when he went there. He said it looked like it was taken from the Old World. It didn't look like anything he'd ever seen in America. What if it really was? What if Dorian somehow moved a stone circle from there to here?"

"It's possible," Gareth mused. "Dorian is fairly ancient himself and one of the strongest warlocks I've ever met. That would still be quite an endeavor."

I shook my head. "Not given his unique talents. He can call the forest to his aid."

Sydney's eyes widened. "That's right. He gave you a totem that harnessed his spell. You used it to fight off the Réminians out on the Anderson property."

"Exactly!" I nodded, feeling pretty good about myself. Using Isis' magic was cool and all, but this was Dorian's magic. Something I had before I even knew anything about my past life.

"We ask the forest all around the sanctuary to help. They'll march in there with the stones and put them in place around the warehouse. I'll focus my Isis spell, you know, the cremation power I used before. It'll leave the warehouse an ashy mess, but it'll also form a barrier. Any of those undead try to come through, and *poof.*"

"Plus, you might be able to bring Charlie back," Aiden added. "If the Morrigan leaves his body in the underworld…"

I inhaled deeply. "Maybe. It's worth a shot."

"Only if you can bring him back as he was," Gareth insisted. "Otherwise, he has to stay there. Let him rest in peace."

"Right. He wouldn't want me to bring him back as a killer. But if there's a chance to save him, I'll take it."

Sydney stood, excitement lighting up her eyes. "Let's get to work then. We've got a lot to do if we're going to make this happen."

Gareth grinned. "I knew there was a reason I kept you guys around."

I rolled my eyes. "Yeah, yeah. Don't forget who's the brains of this operation."

We all laughed, the tension in the room easing a bit. Maybe we could pull this off. We could save Charlie and stop the apocalypse. It wouldn't be easy, but nothing worth doing ever is.

CHAPTER TWENTY-ONE

The frigid night air bit at my cheeks as I stumbled through the dark forest, following Gareth's broad silhouette through the maze of gnarled branches. My breath came out in puffs of mist that danced and evaporated before my eyes. The full moon peeked between the barren trees, casting everything in an eerie blue glow.

"Are we close?" Sydney's anxious voice cut through the heavy silence. Her normally perfect blonde hair was a tangled mess from our chaotic teleportation into the woods.

"A little farther," I whispered. These woods held old, primal power, and you didn't go shouting and trampling through them whenever you felt like it.

We entered the stone circle, the monolithic rocks rising from the forest floor like giants frozen in time. I slowed, my shoes crunching on a carpet of dried leaves and twigs. Even Aiden seemed affected, his usual goofy grin replaced by wide-eyed concern as he surveyed the dark woods around us, expecting a walking corpse to attack us from the darkness.

They never came. They weren't focused on the sanctuary. The

resurrected were all moving toward the warehouse, where Balzac summoned them before we sent him packing to the underworld.

I approached the center of the circle reverently, my fingers closing around the small totem on my necklace. Dorian had made it for me, lashing pieces of wood together in an intricate pattern. I willed my magic into it like he had taught me, imagining it flowing from my fingertips.

The power swirled slowly at first. It caressed the circle of standing stones, charging the air. I felt the energy thrumming through me, connecting me to the spirits of this place.

"It's working," Gareth stated behind me, a note of awe in his voice.

I barely heard him, lost in the power. The trees seemed to bend toward me, softly creaking as if whispering secrets only I could hear. This place remembered me. It remembered *us*. And it would help.

I closed my eyes, letting my consciousness expand outward until I could see the forest through the eyes of the trees. In my mind, I spoke to them directly, my voice ringing through their shared network of roots.

"My friends, I beg you. You are the most ancient protectors of this world. You are the stalwart guardians of the Earth. I need your help. We need to move this sanctuary."

In answer, a crack of thunder shook the ground beneath my feet. My eyes flew open as, all around, the trees began to move. Their thick roots ripped from the earth, undulating like massive tentacles. The trees hauled their immense trunks across the clearing with surprising speed, converging on the circle.

With creaks and groans, they grasped the ancient standing stones, their bark-covered limbs straining. The stones shuddered, briefly resisting before relenting. One by one, the trees wrenched them up, pulling the towering megaliths from their foundations.

I directed the trees as they began shuffling toward the warehouse, their foot-like roots leaving furrows in the loam. "Take the circle," I urged. "Reform it around the warehouse. If you can see it in my mind's eye, through our connection, you know where to go!"

The trees increased their pace, branches waving as if to say they understood. I watched them go, my heart swelling with gratitude and love for these gentle giants.

We'd hiked about a mile through the woods when I felt a familiar presence at my side. I glanced over to see Roy loping along, his shaggy gray fur flickering like smoke. The great spirit wolf's eyes fixed ahead, intent on our goal.

On my other side padded Smoky, the wise old spirit bear. Though I couldn't touch them in their non-corporeal forms, having these powerful spirits accompany us on the journey filled me with courage.

As we drew closer to the warehouse, the trees slowed, their progress impeded. All around us, the undead were emerging from the shadows. Their moans and shuffling footsteps surrounded us. I counted at least thirty, and more were approaching by the second.

Aiden lifted his shotgun and blasted the head off the nearest corpse with a deafening boom. It collapsed, truly dead once more. Gareth and Sydney began hurling concussive spells, sending the undead flying back.

I focused my power, drawing on my ancient magic. With a thrust of will, I disintegrated five of the foul things, reducing them to swirling ash. Roy and Smokey also took physical form. They drew on my power to do it and fought off any undead who got near me. They were my bodyguards. Damn good at it, too. Yet no matter how many of the dead I destroyed, more kept coming.

"We have to keep moving!" I yelled. The trees had come to a complete halt, unable to push through the ever-growing horde. I swallowed back my panic. If we didn't break through soon, we'd be overwhelmed.

Then, a flash of light nearly blinded me. I threw up a hand to shield my eyes. When I lowered it, I gasped.

Dorian stood beside me, looking as gorgeous as ever. He held an ornately carved staff with ancient Egyptian symbols etched along its length. Before I could react, he swung it overhead. A shockwave of energy erupted outward, sending the undead flying back, clearing a wide swath through their ranks.

"Dorian!" I couldn't contain my excitement. I started toward him, but he held up a hand.

"No time for reunions, my love." His voice was cool and calm despite the chaos around us. "You must press onward. I will hold them off."

With another sweeping gesture, he sent more creatures flying. The trees began shuffling forward again. I tore my gaze from Dorian. As much as I wanted to run into his arms, he was right. We had a mission to complete. I nodded and kept moving, Roy and Smoky at my side. Dorian parted the sea of undead like Moses at the Red Sea.

We were getting close to the warehouse now. Gunshots cracked as Aiden blasted away at any undead that stumbled too close. Sydney and Gareth slung spells left and right, keeping the area around us clear. With Dorian clearing the path, our job was a lot easier.

"We're almost there!" I called as much to motivate myself as the others. "Only a little farther!"

We pressed on. The trees fanned out, surrounding the building, as I had instructed.

I planted my feet and called to the trees. "Reform the sanctuary. The whole warehouse must lie within it."

With one thundering *thud* after another, the trees replanted the stones.

As the last stone fell into place, I released my magic into the circle. White energy swirled like a tornado over the warehouse, stretching high into the clouds. Then, the vortex turned a subtle shade of gray. The ash of the undead who were still inside the warehouse.

"We freaking did it!" I wrapped my arms around Dorian. "I can't believe you're here!"

I heard Gareth release a sigh. As close as we'd gotten, he knew my heart always belonged to Dorian. Reluctantly, he approached and extended his hand to Dorian. "Thank you, Dorian."

Dorian recoiled. "I'm sorry. I cannot shake your hand. Connecting with others…I'm still cursed."

Gareth nodded and stepped back. "Except with Briar. You can touch her."

Dorian nodded. "She's the exception to the rule. I believe it's because I was tasked by Osiris to be her guardian."

I glanced at the crook dangling from Dorian's waist. Back when I'd first learned I was Isis, Osiris appeared in a ghostly form and gave the hooked staff to Dorian. He could use it to help guide me and focus my Isis power. I wasn't sure if I still needed it, but his presence made me feel stronger and more in control. Still totally myself.

As we stood there, catching our breath and enjoying the peace that finally settled around us, I felt Dorian's hand brush against mine. It was a light touch, almost fleeting, but it sent shivers down my spine. I lost my breath, my heart hammering.

"Dorian," I whispered, my voice barely audible above the rustling of the trees.

He turned to me, his gaze intense. "Briar," he replied, his voice low and husky.

Without another word, we leaned in, our lips meeting in a searing kiss. It was like nothing else existed in the world but him and me. His arms wrapped around me, pulling me close, and I melted into his embrace.

It was like coming home, like finding the missing piece of

myself I never knew I'd lost. I was complete with him, and I never wanted to let him go.

Yet, as always, reality intruded. We still had to get inside the circle and into the warehouse.

Roy and Smoky nudged us apart, reminding us of our task. I drew a deep breath, trying to quell the longing that still burned within me. We stepped inside the circle, the energy of it pulsing beneath our feet.

The warehouse door stood before us, a metal behemoth that looked like it had weathered many storms. I reached out, my hand trembling with anticipation.

Dorian placed his hand over mine, steadying me. "Together," he murmured.

We pushed the door open, revealing a dark, foreboding space. A rank odor assaulted my senses, and I had to fight the urge to retch.

Then, something moved in the shadows. A flicker of movement so quick I almost missed it.

"Dorian," I whispered, my hand tightening on his. "I think there's something in here."

He nodded, his eyes fixed on the darkness. "Stay close," he warned. "Whatever it is, your magic can't kill it."

That was when he emerged. Just as he'd appeared before when he gave me the Book of the Dead. Anubis, his jackal head glaring at me with red, glowing, beady eyes.

"Isis, what are you doing?"

"Saving the fucking world," I retorted. "What are you doing?"

"It has been foretold! This is the end of days. Who are you to interfere?"

I shrugged. "I'm Briar, bitch."

Dorian touched my arm. I felt an extra surge of power courtesy of the crook dangling from his waist.

With a fierce cry, Anubis lunged at us. Dorian stepped

forward, his staff ready, but Anubis was too quick. In the blink of an eye, he had closed the distance, his razor-sharp claws extended.

I was ready for him, though. I channeled my power into a beam of white-hot energy, aiming directly for his chest. The blast hit him dead-on, knocking him back several feet. But he didn't stay down for long.

With a snarl, he charged us again, his claws slashing through the air. Dorian swung his staff upward, deflecting the blow. I followed up with another blast of energy, forcing Anubis back again.

His eyes burned like hot coals. "You cannot stop what is coming, Isis. The end of days is inevitable."

"We'll see about that," I shot back.

We continued our battle, each exchanging blows, neither giving an inch. Anubis was powerful, but my magic was stronger. Dorian's guidance and support only bolstered me further.

With each blow, my exhaustion increased. I didn't know how much longer I could keep going, but I couldn't give up. Not when the fate of the world was at stake.

Anubis lunged at me again, and I barely dodged out of the way. His claws scraped along my arm, drawing blood. I cried out but didn't let the pain distract me. I gathered my power, ready to deliver one final, devastating blow.

Before I could, Anubis released a piercing howl and disappeared.

I gasped, clutching my bleeding arm. "What the hell happened?"

Dorian shook his head, looking as confused as I felt. "I don't know, but I have a feeling this isn't over yet."

I nodded, my heart still racing from the battle. As we caught our breath, I couldn't help but feel a sense of unease. Anubis had seemed so sure of himself, so certain the end of days was inevitable. Was there really no stopping it? There had to be. Otherwise, why was he trying to fight us?

"We need to stick to the plan," I announced. "But with Anubis lurking, I can't leave you all here to face him alone."

Gareth drew a deep breath. "We're with you, Briar. Open the portal. It's time to storm the underworld and end this shit."

CHAPTER TWENTY-TWO

The portal to the underworld yawned open before us, a gaping maw of swirling shadows. I peered into its inky depths, half expecting bony fingers to reach out and drag me into oblivion.

"No sign of Anubis yet," Gareth muttered, gaze darting around the empty warehouse. "That doesn't mean he won't try to trap us down there."

"Well, we can't stand here with our thumbs up our asses," I insisted. "Time to nut up or shut up."

I steeled myself and stepped toward the portal. A hand grabbed my arm, stopping me short. Dorian.

"I've got an idea," he stated. One of his tattoos glowed with a violet energy, a power I'd never seen him use before. What had happened to him in Egypt? Something was different about his magic, but if it helped, I could get the details later. The air crackled with power as he called upon the magic of the stone circle outside. A shimmering barrier formed around the portal's entrance.

"There. That should keep even a god like Anubis from shutting this thing behind us." Dorian smirked, clearly pleased with himself.

"Damn," I remarked. "Impressive. What kind of magic was that?"

Dorian sighed. "It's nothing to worry about. A long story. A lot has changed since I left, Briar."

"Changed?" I raised an eyebrow.

Dorian shook his head. "Not my feelings for you. I met some interesting netters. I learned a few things."

I gave Dorian's hand a grateful squeeze. "All right. Let's get this over with." Dorian and I stepped into the swirling vortex of shadows with my friends close behind. Here we went again, marching into the belly of the beast.

We emerged into a wasteland. Miles of barren, rocky terrain stretched in every direction under a bleak gray sky. No signs of life anywhere, not even a scrap of vegetation. It was the kind of place that sucked all the hope right out of your soul.

I shivered, memories of this forsaken realm churning to the surface. Once, this had been the dwelling place of millions of souls. Now, nothing but a vacant shell remained.

"This is all kinds of fucked up," I muttered.

"Set's doing, no doubt," Dorian commented, his face grim. "Stripped the underworld bare when he drew them out."

I shook my head. "This wasn't all his work. We played a role. We were the ones who broke the veil to begin with."

"This place isn't totally empty," Gareth reminded us. "Set himself is lurking around here somewhere. The Morrigan, too."

I nodded. "And Charlie. Can't forget about him."

I closed my eyes, trying to access the remnants of Isis' memories. They came in fractured pieces, blurred images, and feelings rather than anything coherent. However, I found a sense of direction, an invisible tether pulling me forward.

I opened my eyes. "This way. I think."

We set off across the desolate landscape. The ground was rough and uneven, making the going slow. More than once, someone stumbled over the rocks, but no one complained. We were all too focused on our goal.

After what felt like hours, a towering shape appeared on the horizon. An ancient pyramid, its edges smoothed by time but still conveying a sense of enormity.

"There." A surge of recognition hit me. "That's where we'll find Osiris."

We picked up the pace, moving quickly across the broken ground. Anticipation thrummed through the group. We approached the pyramid cautiously, wary of any traps or guardians that might be lurking, but the entrance stood open and unguarded. I glanced back at the others.

"Be ready for anything," I told them.

We stepped inside.

The interior was dim, lit only by a few scattered torches. As my eyes adjusted, I made out a towering shape on a dais at the far end. A throne, and on it sat the unmistakable form of a mummy.

I crept forward, my senses straining. This had to be Osiris, but something felt off. Powerful magic hung in the air, obscuring my attempts to get a clear read.

As I drew closer, the figure on the throne didn't react. I reached out a hand tentatively and touched its linen-wrapped arm. Still no response.

I closed my eyes, focusing intently. The magic clouding my senses peeled back. What I sensed beneath wasn't the raw power of a god. It was the flickering life force of a mortal man.

My eyes snapped open. "This isn't Osiris. It's a man under some kind of enchanted sleep." I stepped back, my mind racing. "Osiris isn't here."

Dread crept up my spine. Where was he, and what state might we find him in? The situation had gotten a lot more complicated.

"Where the hell is he?" Sydney asked, coming up beside me.

I shook my head. "I don't know, but Set's killed him before. He must have done something to Osiris again."

My hands curled into fists. That bastard somehow got to Osiris first, but why take him and leave this mortal in his place? It didn't make any sense.

I began unwinding the linen strips that swathed the figure. As the last layer fell away, I stumbled back with a gasp.

It was Charlie.

My fingers trembled as I reached to touch his face. His skin was cool under my fingertips. When I brushed his cheek, his eyes flew open. He jerked upright with a choking gasp like a drowning man breaking the surface.

"Charlie!" I cried. "You're alive!"

He blinked at me in confusion, chest heaving. "Briar? What… how did I get here?"

I threw my arms around him, relief leaving me giddy. He was alive. I didn't know how he'd wound up here, and right now, I didn't care.

Charlie awkwardly patted my back. "Hey, it's okay. I'm all right."

I pulled back, getting a hold of myself. There would be time for questions later. First, I had to make sure this was actually Charlie.

"Charlie, is it really you?" I asked urgently. "Or is the Morrigan still inside?"

He shook his head. "No, it's me. She left my body as soon as we got here."

I studied his face, looking for any hint of deception. His eyes were clear, his expression open and guileless. This was my Charlie.

I blew out a breath. "Okay. Do you remember what happened? How did you end up here?"

Charlie rubbed his temples. "It's fuzzy. I remember the Morrigan bringing me here. Then she just…left. Next thing I knew, Set was standing over me. He said something about teaching Osiris a lesson." Charlie's eyes widened. "Osiris! Where is he?"

I shook my head grimly. "We don't know. He's gone, and Set did something to you, too. Do you remember anything else?"

Charlie squeezed his eyes shut, thinking hard. After a moment, he shook his head helplessly. "No, that's all I've got. The last clear memory is Set leaning over me, then it goes black."

My heart sank. We still had no idea what Set had done to Osiris or where he might be. At least Charlie was safe. I would unravel this mystery soon enough. For now, we had to find Osiris. How could we do that in an underworld so large, so vast, that it housed every soul of every person who'd ever died?

One way or another, we'd find a way.

CHAPTER TWENTY-THREE

The sulfurous stench hit me like a punch to the gut as we marched through the smoldering wasteland. Flames licked at jagged rocks jutting up from the parched earth. Dorian trudged beside me, his brow furrowed in concentration as he clutched his staff and crook. I grazed his arm, focusing my power. A jolt zapped through me, and suddenly, the crook glowed brighter. Yet I still couldn't sense Osiris.

I shook my head. "That crook's about as helpful here as a screen door on a submarine. I'm getting nothing."

Dorian scowled. "I don't think the crook's the problem. If you can't find Osiris—"

I sighed. "It means he's not here."

Aiden grunted. The atmosphere was clearly taking a greater toll on him since he lacked magic. "Where the hell could he be, then?"

I shrugged. "Beats me, but traipsing around this godforsaken place isn't getting us any closer."

I wiped the sweat from my brow and looked back at the others. Gareth's perfect hair was plastered to his forehead, Sydney fanned herself with a hand, and Aiden trudged along like a mule. Only Charlie seemed unfazed, the lucky duck. His extended nap, or perhaps his druidic magic, gave him more vigor than the rest of us. Including me.

"I reckon we need to rethink this plan," I stated. "Before we all melt into puddles."

A dark shadow passed overhead. I glanced up, shielding my eyes from the harsh red glow of the underworld sky. A raven circled above us, its wings spread wide.

"Hey!" Charlie called. "I know that bird."

The raven swooped lower before landing gracefully on a withered tree nearby. Its form shimmered, feathers melting into pale flesh and flowing black hair. The Morrigan stood before us, regarding me with her piercing violet eyes.

"What happened?" I asked. "Where are Set and Osiris?"

The Morrigan tilted her head. "Set has taken Osiris to Duat."

"Duat?" Gareth echoed.

I nodded, memories of my past life surfacing. "It's the realm of the Egyptian gods. Like their home base." I met the Morrigan's gaze. "Set must be trying to get back in. Probably using Osiris as leverage. He was banished ages ago for what he did to Osiris."

Aiden scratched his head. "How do we get there?"

"There must be a portal somewhere in the underworld," I remarked. "Did you see where Set went?"

The Morrigan considered me. "I know where the portal lies. First, you must fulfill your promise."

I tensed. Right. My promise to give up my resurrection powers if she helped mend the veil between the living and the dead. But if Set succeeded, none of it would matter.

"I'll give it up after the world's not ending," I stated firmly. "The deal was I'd give it to you when we fixed the veil. That ain't done yet."

The Morrigan bowed her head. "Very well, Isis."

Dorian frowned. "Briar, you can't hand over your magic."

"It's the only way to fix things," I insisted. "Powers like mine…

no one should have them. She isn't asking for my normal power. Not what I always had. Only my power to bring back the dead. Nothing good comes of it."

The Morrigan nodded slowly. "Very well. Follow me." She transformed back into a raven and took flight. We hurried after her shadow, delving deeper into the wasteland.

We followed the Morrigan through the barren wasteland, our footsteps echoing off the jagged rocks. The air felt heavy, like a storm was brewing, even though the sky was empty and vast.

After what seemed like hours, we came upon a cliff over-looking a churning river of souls. Their warped faces danced under the surface. Across the river was an obsidian palace, its spires piercing the gloomy sky. Ancient hieroglyphics carved into the walls seemed to shift and move before my eyes.

"Set's portal lies within," the Morrigan announced, alighting on a boulder. "However, the way is perilous. The river will attempt to claim any who cross."

"What's up with the souls in the river?" I asked. "I thought everyone got resurrected."

"They were not whole," the Morrigan explained. "These spirits in the river are what the resurrected lack. Their true humanity."

Aiden chuckled. "Is this where Osiris's wiener was lost?"

I tilted my head. "I suppose it is. It's like the Nile of the under-world. Where Set first cast Osiris the first time he killed him."

Aiden gulped. "I'm not touching that water. I don't want to lose my dick!"

I laughed. "Or your soul. I'd be more worried about that."

Aiden shook his head. "Look, I don't use my soul much, but my johnson is a big part of who I am."

Sydney giggled. "Emphasis on the big."

I winced. "I really don't want to know."

"Will you brave the waters or not?" the Morrigan asked.

This was a true test. Still, we had to stop Set before he could wreak more havoc.

"I'll go first." Gareth rolled up his sleeves.

I grabbed his arm. "Like hell you will." I turned to the Morrigan. "There's got to be another way across."

She blinked her beady eyes. "I know of no other way. Perhaps *together,* you can find one."

"I have an idea," Charlie piped up. "Follow me."

Charlie sauntered over to the river's edge and stripped down to nothing.

"Full moon's out tonight," Aiden jested.

I chuckled. The next thing I knew, Charlie dove into the water and shifted in mid-air, taking the form of a giant whale. He flailed around the shoreline.

"I think he wants to give us a ride," Gareth added.

I nodded and stepped toward Charlie. He was massive. Could have swallowed Jonah. Or Pinocchio.

"Hey, Charlie!" Aiden called. "Be careful. If you see a worm in the water, it's probably a god's wanker."

Charlie puffed some water from his blow hole.

I glanced at Aiden. "Be careful. Don't touch the water."

Aiden nodded. "Got it. Not going to risk it!"

I climbed onto Charlie's back, feeling the smooth skin under my hands as I settled into position. The others followed suit, with Aiden clinging tightly to Charlie's dorsal fin and Sydney grasping his tail. Gareth wedged between Charlie's massive fins, his hair whipping around his face as we moved out into the swirling current of souls. Dorian held onto my waist.

As we moved farther into the river, I felt the souls tug at my essence, like an ethereal force trying to pull me off Charlie and under the surface. It wasn't strong. More like a gentle tug. "Stay focused, everyone!" I shouted. "Don't give in to the urges you're feeling."

"They can't have my dick!" Aiden shouted. "Not gonna happen! No way in hell!"

We reached the other side, gasping but alive. Charlie dove deep into the water, then shot himself out before flopping onto the beach. He shifted again into his usual form.

"Sorry guys. Still naked."

I chuckled. "No worries. That was brilliant. But Charlie?"

He tilted his head.

"What about your soul? Did you lose something in there?"

Charlie frowned. "I don't know. I can't tell."

"Well, we aren't leaving without you."

"Briar, I told you before—"

"I said we aren't leaving without you. If your soul is in this river, I'll fish it out of there if it's the last thing I do."

Charlie pressed his lips together and nodded but didn't speak.

I turned toward the megalith in front of us. The obsidian palace loomed before us, its doors wide open.

"Let's go," I insisted, my voice low and determined.

When we stepped inside, the whole place glowed with multi-colored lights emanating from dozens of portals. Most of them shone golden, like the sun. One stood out from the rest with pure white light.

"What are we looking at here?" Sydney asked.

"Those golden portals go back to Earth," I stated. "It's like holes in the Swiss cheese of the veil between life and death. They're how all those people left before. My guess? They had to cross the river to do it and left their souls behind. That's why they came back like they are."

"Makes sense." Gareth nodded. "The white portal. Is that…"

"The Duat," I commented with a resolute nod. "I know it. I remember it. That's where we're going."

CHAPTER TWENTY-FOUR

The Duat hit me like a blast furnace. One second, I was in the chilly underworld. The next, I was sweating my ass off in the sweltering halls of the Egyptian home of the gods.

"What the actual fu—"

I blinked against the blinding sunlight reflecting off golden walls covered in hieroglyphs and intricate carvings. This was no dark, spooky underworld. It was straight out of an archeology textbook. Or Indiana Jones' wet dream.

Ahead of me, Ra rose from his throne, looking like a human lightbulb. His skin glowed so bright it was hard to make out his features. Two figures stood before him, their forms washed out by Ra's brilliance.

"Alas, the rematch can finally happen now that all are present," the sun god announced.

"Come again?" I asked, squinting at the god of gods.

One of the two figures turned. Horus, his falcon head making him look like a character from the cringiest furry convention ever. Still, he was my son.

"Set wishes to challenge me once more for my throne," he explained.

"Uh, okay?" I hedged. "Why are *we* here?"

Then it hit me, a tidal wave of memories crashing over me. I staggered under the force of thousands of years of history flooding my mind.

I saw myself aiding Horus during the first challenge, helping him cheat against Set because Set was cheating, too. Yet when it came time to kill Set, I had shown mercy and spared his life.

Horus saw this as a betrayal. In his rage, he killed me. His own mother. That was why I had died as the goddess Isis and been reincarnated centuries later. It's why I became Briar Bloom.

"I made a grave mistake," Horus admitted softly, approaching me. His falcon head dipped in shame.

"You think?" I snapped.

Set laughed coldly. "Horus was never fit to rule. Killing his own mother in a tantrum? Pathetic."

I held up a hand. "Enough. The past is done. What matters now is the present." I turned my gaze on Set. "You've brought great evil into this world by calling forth the dead and emptying the underworld. Then, you abducted Osiris. You deserve no throne."

Set's red eyes narrowed. "Yet here I stand, ready to issue another challenge. Perhaps you should reconsider where your loyalties lie, Isis. If you side with me in the trials, we can return to Earth and rule together. Death need no longer have a hold on anyone. We can raise everyone!"

I met his glare steadily. "With warped souls? No, I don't think so. My loyalty is to protecting the mortal realm from petty grudges like yours. This rivalry ends today."

Horus shifted uneasily. "Mother…"

"No," I stated firmly. "I won't be drawn into the past again. I'm ending this, once and for all."

I strode forward, magic crackling at my fingertips. Goddess or not, it was time to kick some ancient Egyptian ass.

Ra held up a hand, his form blazing bright. "Peace, Isis. Violence will not end this cycle."

I stopped short, clenching my fists. "Then what will? This pointless feud has gone on long enough."

Ra regarded me solemnly. "What is your purpose in coming here?"

I inhaled deeply, calming myself. "I was reborn as a mortal woman. I have no intention of remaining here. My place is on Earth now, protecting it from threats like this." I waved a hand at Horus and Set. "Petty rivalries that span millennia, feuds that never end. It has to stop."

Ra nodded. "And so it shall, but the path must be walked wisely." He studied me for a long moment. "You have grown much in wisdom since your days as a goddess. Perhaps you can end what was begun so long ago."

I hoped he was right. The fate of two realms depended on it.

Ra turned to me. "You wish to see Osiris. I must warn you, he is not well. What Set did to him…"

My heart seized. "Please, I must see him."

Ra nodded slowly. "Very well, but your friends must remain here." He raised his hand, and a portal opened in the crystalline wall.

I turned to Dorian, squeezing his hand. "I'll be back soon. Don't go starting any trouble while I'm gone."

He smirked. "No promises." His eyes were worried.

Ra led me through the shimmering portal into a dimly lit chamber. My breath caught at the sight of Osiris.

He lay unwrapped from his linen bindings, his strong body a ruin of knotted scars and misshapen limbs. Only his face remained unchanged, still noble and handsome as I remembered when I saw him in my past life's memories. I went to him, kneeling by his side. At my touch, his dark eyes fluttered open.

"Isis," he murmured. "My love, you've returned."

Tears pricked my eyes. "I'm here," I whispered, stroking his cheek. A thousand memories of our life together flooded through me. Our laughter, our passion, the blissful days we'd shared as husband and wife.

Grief and anger warred within me. What had Set done to the man I loved? I would make it right, whatever it took.

I leaned down and pressed my lips to his in a desperate, sorrowful kiss.

Osiris gently pulled back. "Our love belongs to another life, my dear. Your heart now belongs to another."

I blinked in confusion before understanding lit within me. Dorian.

Osiris gave a faint smile. "The warlock carries my crook now. He is the one I chose to ascend and defeat Set and Horus. To do so as your suitor, as your future husband."

"But Horus is my son," I protested weakly. "I won't hurt him! Even if he did lop my head off my shoulders once."

"I know your gentle heart, Isis. You need not kill the boy, only best him." Osiris winced, shifting against the stone slab. "Ra will dictate the trial."

I swallowed hard. "The Morrigan demanded my power in exchange for her aid. I need another god to heal the veil."

Osiris grunted, forcing himself upright. "There's a good reason that raven is deemed vile among our people. She is no evil goddess, yet neither is she kind. If the Morrigan gains your abilities, she could twist all souls in the underworld. We would have no say at all about the souls in the life thereafter."

I shivered at the thought, my shoulders slumping. Still, we needed help. "Then what can be done? The veil is torn, and the worlds bleed together. Anubis himself tried to stop me from coming here."

At the jackal god's name, Osiris' face darkened. "Yes. He believes this damage will further his apocalypse. He's been looking forward to that day since he was born among us, the child of Ra and Hesat."

I sighed. "That's right. It's all coming back to me. Ra doesn't share Anubis' ambitions, though."

"Ra knows, as we all do, that all things must come to an end in time. The question is, is that time now or later?"

I huffed. "I won't let the world end. Not now. Not ever."

Osiris inclined his head. "Someday, it must happen. It is inevitable. However, you can delay it. If you and your warlock defeat Set and Horus, claiming the throne, Anubis will have no choice but to relent. To delay his end of days once more."

Hope flickered inside me as Osiris continued. "Together, you and Dorian can heal the veil. He's already begun his ascent."

"When he went to Egypt?" I asked.

"He met other powerful magicians who saw my crook in his hand. They granted him the power of the pharaohs, but his ascent is not complete. You must overcome those who would challenge him. You must aid Dorian against his challengers."

I squared my shoulders, meeting Osiris' gaze. "I won't let them win. Whatever it takes, the apocalypse will be stopped."

Osiris smiled grimly. "Spoken like the goddess you once were. I know you will do what is needed, Isis. You always have."

I exhaled, feeling the weight of destiny settling upon me. With Dorian at my side, I could do this. I had to believe that.

The worlds would not fall into darkness. Not if I had anything to say about it.

"Return to Ra," Osiris told me. "He knows my wishes, but he cannot simply grant you a victory on my behalf. You must earn it. Are you prepared?"

My breath caught. "I don't know. How do we win?"

Osiris grasped my hand. "Set and Horus will cheat. That is their way. Do not do the same. Defeat them with honor, and Ra will marry you, granting you both the honor to represent our family on the Earth. You will be the pharaohs."

CHAPTER TWENTY-FIVE

Leaving Osiris behind in his condition was harder than I expected. The more my old memories came to mind, the more I came to appreciate my past life. Isis might have been a god, but she wasn't the kind of all-powerful, almighty ruler so far beyond humans that her desires and passions weren't relatable. She was more human, even as a goddess, than she ever knew a god could be.

As Isis, I loved. I knew pain and felt the sting of betrayal. Yet something was missing back then that I now understood. As a goddess, I'd still thought myself entitled to whatever I had. Not so anymore. Living as an orphan, working as a waitress, having loved and lost, I knew I couldn't take anything for granted. I was grateful for what I had, for the people in my life, and I cared about them more than anything.

Ra was still seated on his throne, and Set and Horus remained in front of him, awaiting their trials. Ra folded his massive arms over his muscular chest. "Have you made a decision, Isis? Will you fulfill Osiris' wish?"

I lifted my chin. "Damn right. Dorian and I will compete together."

Set took two steps forward. Balzac's bald head reflected Ra's natural radiance so much that I could barely look at him without squinting. "This is preposterous! I came demanding a rematch. This is between Horus and me! Isis can only take my side or his!"

Ra tilted his head. "Why should Isis have to choose to support the one who once killed her husband and wounded him again, and her son, who once betrayed and killed her? Would that be just, Set?"

"It would not," Horus agreed. "If my mother wishes to compete, I do not object. Let her endure the trials with us."

Set barked a harsh laugh. "Please. These trials are a farce, and you know it. Last go-round, Osiris split everything down the middle between me and birdbrain here, then picked his favorite in the end anyway."

Horus gave a solemn nod. "Indeed. If we are to engage in the trials, the results must matter. It is clear Osiris favors his wife Isis and her pet human. The decision cannot fall to him in the end."

Set narrowed his eyes and sneered at me. "What trials will it be this time, Ra? Shall we see who can transform into the mightiest hippopotamus and hold our breath the longest underwater?"

Ra shook his head, the light around him briefly dimming. "Such a trial would prove nothing of worth here. Strength and power may win a physical competition, but it does not make one worthy to rule."

"Perhaps a race then, in boats carved of papyrus?" Horus suggested. "A test of speed and cunning on the Nile?"

"No," Ra stated. "That, too, would not serve our purpose."

Set crossed his massive arms. "Well then, a wrestling match? A spear-throwing contest? Name the physical challenge, and I shall prevail."

Ra regarded him sternly. "You mistake me. This is not a competition of brute force. The trials shall test the heart and mind."

Set and Horus exchanged uncertain glances.

"The trials shall reveal the true nature of each participant," Ra continued. "I see now where the flaw lay in ages past. You sought only to best one another through tricks and deceit. Your rivalry poisoned the trials from the start."

Finally, Ra faced me, his eyes glinting like sunlight on the Nile. "Isis has chosen to share the path with her companion. Set and Horus, would you choose a second?"

Set shook his head. "If I cannot have Isis as my queen, I will share my rule with no one. This is my right, my destiny."

"Likewise," Horus added. "I will not share my rule with another. A ruler must always be wary of sedition, and those closest to the throne are the greatest threat."

"Very well," Ra declared. "The first trial is complete. Isis and Dorian prevail."

Set's eyes flashed with anger. "What deception is this? There was no trial!"

Horus added, "We were given no chance to prove ourselves."

Ra held up a hand. "You proved my point. You both crave power solely for yourselves. Neither of you considered that to share authority demonstrates wisdom and selflessness, qualities required in a just ruler."

He turned to me with an approving smile. "Isis understands that to share power is not to dilute it but to strengthen it. A partnership founded on trust and respect shall endure where a sole despot will falter."

I grinned at Dorian, glad we'd passed the first trial, though my smugness faded at Ra's next words.

"There will be two more trials, each designed to test your character. I hope you have learned from this first failure, Set and Horus. The trials ahead will only grow more difficult."

A nervous pit formed in my stomach. Sure, Dorian and I had aced round one, but three of us were competing. If we split the trials, who would win? We still had to win at least one of the other two.

I squeezed Dorian's hand. "Bring it on," I told Ra with more bravado than I felt. "We're ready."

Dorian and I stood united as Set and Horus muttered their assent. This contest was far from over.

Ra nodded, satisfied. "Very well. Let the second trial commence. Before you begin, a bit of advice. Things are not always as they appear. Be certain of your choice!"

Ra snapped his fingers. A blinding flash enveloped us, and I felt a strange twisting sensation, like falling down a rabbit hole. When the dizziness passed, Dorian and I stood in an ancient Egyptian granary. Sandy stone walls surrounded us, and sunlight streamed through slatted windows near the ceiling. The air smelled of roasted barley and honey.

"This is Egypt, around 2000 BC," Dorian murmured, scanning our surroundings. "During the Middle Kingdom, if I had to guess."

I peeked outside the granary entrance at a small crowd of men. Some of them dressed luxuriously and were accompanied by guards with spears. Others wore dusty kilts and sandals, their faces etched with desperation. As I watched, several came forward pleading for help in Ancient Egyptian. I understood them. Thank you, past-life regression.

"According to the ledger, there's only enough grain stored here for one distribution." Dorian examined a papyrus scroll. "I believe the test is determining who is most worthy to receive it."

My shoulders slumped. Only one? That meant picking who lived and who died.

"Let's hear their petitions," Dorian stated. "Then, we'll make our choice and hope it's the right one."

CHAPTER TWENTY-SIX

The musty scent of ancient grain tickled my nose as I stared at the mountain of emmer wheat. This so-called 'trial' felt more like a history reenactment than a test from the gods.

"See any signs of the Dynamic Duo?" I asked Dorian, scanning the crowd before the table where we sat for Balzac's shiny bald pate or Horus' giant falcon head.

"Doubt it," he muttered, flipping through an ancient-looking ledger. "Pretty sure Ra stuck us each in a different pocket dimension. You know, so we can't sabotage each other."

I tugged at my shirt. The sweat was already building up. I didn't mind sandy places, provided an ocean accompanied the sand. Not like I had a lot of beach experience, apart from the rocky lake beaches of the Ozarks. I also didn't have a lot of experience with desert climates. The heat was oppressive. "Of course. Those two bastards cheated the last time. Makes sense."

Dorian examined the ledger over and over. "This is shockingly short on details. I think that's by design. This may not be a real situation, more like a simulation."

I nodded. "The gods' version of the holodeck on the Enterprise."

Dorian chuckled. "Something like that. It's a good thing they don't have those things in real life. How many people would ruin their lives in fantasy worlds if they could?"

I chuckled. "People already do that. It's called online gaming. I hear you, though. The one thing I know for sure is I wouldn't want to see Aiden's holodeck experience. It certainly wouldn't be like this."

"I can only imagine." Dorian shook his head. "What's the hold-up?"

My stomach rumbled loud enough to echo through the cavernous room.

I cleared my throat. A guard about ten yards ahead was preventing the petitioners from approaching. "Hey, buddy. Soldier man. Why are we sitting around here?"

The guard turned and bowed. "I'm simply waiting until you are ready. Shall I allow the first to approach?"

I stared blankly at the guard before narrowing my eyes and shaking my head. "Duh. Yeah. Should have thought of that."

The guard pulled back a rope that separated our disbursement room from the crowd of petitioners.

I drummed my fingers on the table. "So what's our game plan here? Give all the grain to the guy with the most pathetic story?"

"If only it were that simple." Dorian sighed. "Pretty sure the 'right choice' is less obvious."

Dorian raised an eyebrow as the first petitioner approached. The man's fine silken robe and jeweled rings marked him as nobility.

"My lords." The nobleman bowed. "I come before you desperate and humble, in need of your mercy."

I rolled my eyes. "Let me guess. Despite being totally loaded, your family and servants will starve without this grain?"

The nobleman blinked in surprise but quickly recovered. "You are most perceptive, my lady. While my household may appear prosperous, I support many—"

"Yeah, yeah. They'll all die, we get it." I waved my hand. "Next!"

The nobleman scowled but stepped aside.

I leaned toward Dorian. "Think that was too harsh?"

He shook his head. "We don't have time for long sob stories, but we should at least hear them out before passing judgment."

I nodded for the next man to come forward. He was young, barely more than a boy, with a thin and ragged appearance. As he approached us, he kept his gaze lowered in a show of deference.

"Speak your piece," I prompted gently.

"My lords," he began, his voice hesitant. "I'm a poor farmer with a family to feed. Twelve children, and my wife is ill. We have so little as it is, and this winter has been cruel. Without some extra grain, I don't know how we will survive."

He finally raised his eyes, and I saw the desperation there. Twelve children with a sick mother was a heavy burden for one so young.

"You have my sympathy," I told him. "Raising so many with so little cannot be easy."

"No, my lady. Each day is a struggle."

I studied the ledger. It held no clear instructions on how much grain was allotted, only that we could give one disbursement.

"Dorian, do you think there is any way we could divide the stores?" I asked. "Even a portion could mean life or death for these families."

Dorian's brow furrowed as he examined the ledger. "I see no mention of amounts." He met my eyes, his expression solemn. "I fear we can only choose one."

My heart sank. I turned back to the ragged farmer.

"Please wait with the others while we finish hearing petitions. Your plight weighs heavily on us."

He nodded, resignation in his eyes, and slowly walked away. I watched his thin shoulders slump and had to blink back tears.

One disbursement for all these desperate souls. One life saved while the others suffered. How could any choice be right?

The next petitioner approached with a pronounced limp, leaning heavily on a gnarled wooden cane. As he came closer, I saw his body was a map of scars, evidence of a hard life. He stopped before us and bowed his head respectfully.

"My lady, my lord, I come before you a broken man. I served for many years in the pharaoh's army, defending this kingdom from her enemies. The battles left me ruined, no longer able to wield a spear or plow a field."

He gestured to his scarred frame. "As you can see, my body is shattered. I have a wife and six children who depend on me, but I can provide nothing for them now. Without your mercy, they will starve."

I studied the soldier, taking in his injuries and the quiet dignity with which he bore them. He had sacrificed much for his people. How could we not repay that sacrifice?

"Good sir, we thank you for your service," I told him. "Please go wait with the others while we finish hearing petitions. Your valor has touched us."

Relief flashed across the soldier's face. He bowed again and limped away.

I turned to Dorian, heart aching. "This task grows harder by the moment. So many valid pleas, so much suffering, and only one meager disbursement."

Dorian squeezed my hand, his eyes reflecting my sorrow. No words could encompass our helplessness at that moment. We could only listen and judge as best we could.

I steeled myself as the next petitioner approached.

The man was stooped and frail, leaning heavily on a carved staff. His robe, though clean, was patched and faded. He had the air of a scholar or scribe.

"My lords," he rasped. "I come before you with no tragic story, no threat of starvation. I have lived a long life, raised a family, and now my time grows short. I only ask that you consider those whose need exceeds mine when deciding who shall receive the grain."

I studied the elderly man, surprised by his selflessness. "Friend, would you share some of your story with us? Your life may hold lessons that could guide our choice."

The old man shook his head. "My past deeds are not important. To speak of them would seem like boasting, which does not become me."

A younger man passing by paused and embraced the elder. "Uncle! What brings you here today?"

The old man shrugged. "A small matter. Nothing to concern yourself with."

The younger man turned to us eagerly. "This man saved my life when I was a boy. He took my family into his home during a famine and fed us, though it meant going hungry himself. There is no one in this kingdom more righteous."

As he spoke, other peasants in the granary murmured their agreement. The old man had touched many lives through quiet generosity. My eyes misted as I grasped his hand.

"Sir, your humility is surpassed only by your virtue. We will remember your example as we make our decision."

The grateful chorus of "bless you" from the crowd affirmed we had made the right choice in hearing him. I blinked back tears, praying we would have the wisdom to choose correctly.

I nodded to Dorian. "The poor man's need is most dire. The soldier, though deserving, still has his health to find other ways to provide. This gentleman exemplifies the best in all of us."

Dorian concurred. "A wise choice. The ledger did not specify how much grain, only that there could be one disbursement." He eyed the sacks thoughtfully. "Perhaps if we petition the guard, he might allow a portion for each family."

I glanced at the rigid sentry and headed across the stone floor. He stood resolute, his spear clutched in his grip.

"Good sir, might we have a word? We wish to understand why the stores are so low. With a kingdom this vast, surely there could be more to spare for the people?"

His face softened briefly at my plea before resuming its detached expression.

"You know I cannot make that decision. I simply follow orders to protect what has been set aside."

I touched his arm. "Of course, but you must see the desperation here. Please, help us if you can."

He hesitated, then leaned in and whispered, "The shipments from upriver have been raided, but the vizier does not want panic. I should not have spoken of it."

I squeezed his arm in thanks. There was more here than met the eye.

I approached the table where Dorian sat. "What's the verdict?" he asked. "Any answers that will make this decision simpler?"

I narrowed my eyes. "Perhaps. I think I have an idea."

"What do you suggest?" Dorian asked.

I cleared my throat and called to the guard, the one who'd let the petitioners through at the beginning. "I'd like to visit with the wealthy nobleman, the poor farmer, the soldier, and the wise man who declined to accept his disbursement. Can you bring them to me at once, together?"

The guard bowed his head and left to gather the men. I didn't know if this would work, but we needed a solution. Whatever saved the most lives. That was what we needed to do, but my idea required all of them.

When they gathered, I stood from the table. I approached the poor farmer. "Of all who've approached me today, you have the greatest sympathy. An ill wife and a dozen children. Tell me, why do your fields not provide the bounty needed to feed your family?"

The farmer shook his head. "How can one man care for so

many? Sadly, I've been unable to labor enough in the fields to reap a harvest."

I nodded, then turned to the nobleman. "You have many men in your employ. Tell me, what do they do for you?"

"Why, any sort of labor. They tend gardens, maintain my home, or anything else I require."

"With so many men, why do you not send them to tend gardens that might supply your household with food?"

The nobleman shook his head. "Our ground is not fertile enough to grow what's required. Even with the few gardens we have, the soil brought in from the delta is not enough to provide for the household."

I waved him aside and asked the old soldier to approach. "Tell me, what were your responsibilities when you served the kingdom?"

"I led many men," the soldier stated. "Not always, of course. I worked my way up the ranks from the position of a simple spearman to a commander."

"Yet your injuries make it impossible to labor in a field."

The soldier bowed his head. "Unfortunately, this is true. If I could, I would do the work myself. Alas, my family depends on your disbursements."

I called over the wise man who'd declined his share. "Why do you bring me here?" the man asked. "I've already said I do not wish to take my share. Give it to someone with greater need."

I shook my head. "You have an eye for need and a compassionate heart. My solution requires your oversight."

Dorian nudged me. "Where is all of this going?"

I grinned. "You'll see. Everyone, gather round and hear my decision."

The men stood in front of me in a half-circle. "You, sir, the farmer, have a field but not the means to work it. The nobleman, my apologies for not remembering your name, has many workers who are skilled to work a field. While he cannot work, the soldier knows how to put men to a task and commands respect. Finally?" I gestured at the wise man who'd declined his share. "This man is honest and noble. He can ensure each receives his due when all is said and done."

"What is your decision?" the nobleman asked.

"I will give the disbursement to this wise man, provided you all agree. He will give out the grain as needed. He can be trusted, for he cares more that others are provided for than he does for himself.

"As for the rest, you will work together, for this supply will not last long. The farmer will offer his field so the men in the nobleman's employ might work the field for harvest. The injured soldier cannot work, but he can assign tasks and manage the operation. Finally, the wise man will parse out the harvests to each worker."

The men discussed my proposal. After a few minutes, they approached. The farmer spoke first. "I will allow others to work my field."

The nobleman added, "My men have the skills and tools to reap a fine harvest, for the farmer's fields are vast."

"We all agree," the soldier stated. "I will ensure the operation is efficient."

Finally, the wise man approached. "I will ensure the distribution is fair and just."

I dusted off my hands as the men left to begin their task. Dorian looked at me, laughing. "Are you sure you're only a waitress?"

I winked at Dorian. "Honey, I'm a girl who knows how to get shit done. When the summer season comes around at Charlie's, we have to be creative to keep up with it all. Everyone sticks to what they do best, and we get through the day."

"You're not only a waitress," Dorian added. "You're also a goddess, apparently."

I shrugged. "Meh. That's beside the point. The old Isis wouldn't have seen this solution."

Dorian hugged me. "Well, let us hope Ra is as impressed as he should be. If he is, that's two out of three. There will be no need for a third trial."

CHAPTER TWENTY-SEVEN

The world around me blinked from existence. I vanished from the dusty Egyptian granary to appear in a massive golden hall with pillars rising on all sides and hieroglyphs etched into every surface.

Dorian stood beside me. Before either of us could get our bearings, a booming voice echoed through the chamber.

"Welcome back, my children."

I craned my neck and spotted the sun god Ra lounging on his ridiculous oversized throne.

"You all faced the same trial, and each of you chose different-ly," Ra continued, shooting pointed looks at the two figures on either side of Dorian and me. Set and Horus, the Beavis and Butthead of the Egyptian pantheon. "Now, we shall see whose choice was the wisest."

Ra lifted his hand, and a beam of light shot from his palm, displaying some kind of magical video replay against the far wall. Pretty impressive. I had to wonder if he broadcasted in HD.

Set crossed his arms, staring daggers at Ra. Yeah, he definitely wasn't thrilled about this little show-and-tell session, either. This wasn't the kind of trial he'd expected, but it was done. If we won, we'd have him and Horus bested, two out of three. I felt good about our decision, but Ra would judge us as he saw fit. There was no telling what he'd decide. From what I remembered of Ra, he was as unpredictable as he was powerful.

I glanced at Dorian, who gave me a subtle nod.

Ra waved his hand, and the first image played across the stone wall.

"Lord Set," Ra stated. "Tell us why you chose to give the grain to the wealthy nobleman."

Set lifted his chin. "A man of means knows how to manage his affairs. He lacked the greatest need but was most able to handle the disbursement effectively. The others lacked the resources to claim the disbursement and take it home. He was the obvious choice."

I rolled my eyes. Set was a good bullshitter, I'd give him that. Truth was, he wanted to suck up to the guy with the most power and influence.

The magical video continued, showing the nobleman accepting the bounty from Set with a gracious bow. Then it flashed to a scene of the nobleman throwing a lavish feast, with musicians and dancers entertaining his guests as they gorged themselves. Meanwhile, the servants received a pittance.

My lips curled in disgust. Within a single night, all the grain was gone, used to satisfy their gluttony while ordinary people starved.

The video faded out, and Ra shook his head. "You have chosen poorly, Set."

Set scowled but said nothing. I felt a small spark of schadenfreude at seeing him dressed down.

Still, I had a feeling Ra was just getting warmed up. Our trial wasn't over yet. Dorian and I would soon have to face judgment for our own choices. I prayed we'd chosen more wisely than Set.

Ra turned his piercing gaze on Horus. "Now, my son, let us examine your choice."

Horus lifted his chin, his gaze steady as Ra's magic projected another scene. It showed the poor farmer Horus had gifted, grinning as he loaded bags of grain onto a mule cart.

I chewed my lip. Looked like Horus chose someone in real need, at least.

The projection skipped ahead, showing the farmer meeting another man on the road. My stomach dropped as I took in the stranger's crude clothes and the wicked gleam in his eyes. Every instinct screamed he was bad news.

When the farmer turned his back, the rogue clubbed him over the head. As the farmer crumpled, the thief made off with the mule carts laden with grain.

The scene shifted again, showing the farmer's ill wife and children huddled together, weeping over his corpse. With the grain stolen, they faced starvation. Now they had lost their provider as well.

The projection faded. Horus looked stricken.

Ra sighed heavily. "A noble effort, my son, but you put the man at risk. Had you asked a few questions and investigated the situation, you'd know the lack of disbursements for all was not on account of famine but due to thieves. The poor man had no means to defend himself. His blood is on your hands."

Horus' face tightened with shame. I felt a pang of sympathy for him, but this was the cold truth of the trial. Even good intentions couldn't change the ruthless consequences of our choices. I'd nearly made the same choice myself.

Ra turned to me next, his blazing eyes ancient and inscrutable. "Isis. Let us see the fruit of your labors."

My mouth went dry. This was it, the moment of reckoning for Dorian and I. Our future and the fate of the world hung in the balance. At least if we failed, we'd have a third opportunity. I drew a deep breath and steadied my nerves. Besides, I felt damn good about what we did. Still, were there any consequences to my decision I couldn't foresee? I was about to find out.

Ra raised his hand. A new projection sprang from his palm, illuminating the throne room.

It showed the wise man from the village receiving the bags of grain I'd given him. His wrinkled face was somber as the other men pooled their resources to help transport them to the poor man's farm.

Set made a derisive noise. "A fine choice, Isis." His voice was thick with sarcasm. "The man didn't even want the blasted grain. He gave it to the farmer, who will meet the same fate in the end as he did when Horus chose him."

"All you've done is pass the buck," Horus accused. "Too cowardly to choose yourself."

Their words prickled my pride. Before I could retort, Ra silenced them with a look.

"Peace. There is more going on here than you suppose."

The projection moved forward in time. Now, the wise man stood before the other men. They accompanied him as he brought the grain to the farmer's field. They passed by the thief on the road, who turned away at seeing the large company surrounding the cart.

The scene flashed forward to show the nobleman's men arriving to work the farmer's field. The soldier managed the operation well, and the man I chose continued to ration the bounty to all.

They had a plentiful harvest. Men worked the fields while children played, and women cooked a great feast. There was more than enough for all.

As the projection faded, I met Ra's gaze evenly. "I chose someone the people trusted, who would ensure everyone was provided for. I charged them to work together so they might all benefit."

Ra inclined his head. Though brief, his smile warmed me like the rising sun.

"You have done well, Isis. Your wisdom has prevailed."

"That's cheating!" Set protested, balling his fists. "The challenge was to choose one petitioner over the others."

"Not so," Ra corrected mildly. "The instructions were to make a choice from among them. Isis chose the wise man to distribute the grain, a man known for fairness, compassion, and good sense. There was even a witness to attest to the man's character. She then empowered the people to provide for themselves. Behold the results."

He waved his hand, and a new scene materialized. A farmer's field, ripe with harvest. The nobleman's men worked the soil while the soldier directed. The wise man weighed out and distributed the bounty. "What you see now is a year later. Isis' decision provided for all and continued to do so for years to come."

Horus glanced at me. "Impressive, Mother."

I grinned. "Thanks!"

"Furthermore," Ra added. "Men who'd normally have nothing to do with one another came together to meet a common need that benefitted all. This would not have happened had it not been for Isis and her wisdom."

I allowed myself a small smile. After the misery Set and Horus' choices had wrought, it was a relief to see people thriving.

Set scowled, unmoved. "A technicality. You bent the rules."

"I used waitress smarts," I replied evenly. "Things get busy, you get overwhelmed, you have to divide and conquer to get the job done. This ain't rocket science, Set. It's common sense. Not like you'd see it."

Set sneered. "Spare me the sentiment."

"Isis and Dorian are the victors," declared Ra. "That is two out of three. There's no need to proceed further."

Set stomped his feet and approached me.

"What do you want, Balzac? You lost, fair and square."

"This isn't over," he growled. "I won't accept it. This was my challenge, my chance for a rematch against Horus, and you interfered, you bitch!"

He spat when he shouted the B-word, his saliva striking my cheek. I wiped it off with the back of my hand. Behind him, Horus seethed. "Leave her be! She won fairly. We had every opportunity to make the same choices but lacked the foresight to do so."

I met Set's glare. "Stand aside. It's over. The only choice you have now is will you help me stop the apocalypse, or will I have to make you do it?"

Set laughed. "You can't make me do anything."

Quick as a viper, he grabbed Charlie and Aiden. Aiden cried out in alarm. "Let go of me, Ball Sack! Briar, help!"

Before I could react, the three vanished in a swirl of inky smoke.

"Damn it!" I screamed. Beside me, Dorian tensed.

"The River Styx," Ra announced grimly. "Set means to drown them in the water, to take their souls to punish you."

My blood turned to ice. We'd barely made it across that damn river. Then again, Charlie dove right in and was fine. Maybe he'd already lost his soul. Perhaps he had special druid magic that protected him. Either way, we had to hurry. Aiden was vulnerable, at least.

I turned to Ra, desperation clawing my throat.

"Help us," I pleaded. "We have to stop Set before he murders them."

The sun god nodded gravely. "Go. Do what must be done to protect your friends and save the world."

I took another step forward. "I need to use Set to save the world. I have to create a dimension, perhaps like the one we entered for the trial. He will lure the dead there if we can trap him inside."

Ra bowed his head. "You have earned what you need. My power is yours."

A bright light shone from Ra's eyes and settled on Dorian and me. A warmth spread through my body. "Thank you, Ra."

Ra nodded. "What comes next, if you will truly save your world, is up to you. Use my power well."

That was all I needed. Dorian and I rushed from the temple, a new urgency fueling our steps. *Hang on, Charlie, Aiden. We're coming.*

CHAPTER TWENTY-EIGHT

We left Ra's throne room. Dorian and I led the charge, Gareth and Sydney not far behind, as we approached the shore of the River Styx.

Set was there but no longer as Balzac. He wasn't the pudgy, balding man I knew. He'd assumed his ancient form.

Shitballs.

The giant red bastard held my bro and Charlie by their necks over the River Styx. When I said giant, I meant the dude was easily ten feet tall with muscles that would make The Rock weep into his protein shake.

Set's voice boomed, loud as thunder. "Isis! Bow down before me and surrender the power you conned from Ra, or the river will consume your dear brother and friend!"

Aiden struggled in Set's grip, face turning purple. "Kick him in the nards, sis!" he choked out. "Right in Balzac's ball sack. I'm sure they're massive targets now!"

I glanced back at Dorian and Gareth. Both shook their heads. As much as it gutted me to see Aiden and Charlie like that, we couldn't let the chaos-loving bastard get his mitts on Ra's power.

Who knew what kind of havoc he'd unleash? Probably turn the Lake of the Ozarks into a giant Jell-O mold or something.

"I can't do that, Set," I hollered at the hulking red god. "You really want me to damn their souls just to save their mortal butts for a hot second? If the apocalypse continues, they'll die soon anyway. Then they'll come back here and lose their souls in the river anyway if they try to escape back to Earth."

Set's bellow nearly blew my eardrums. "I care not for their fates or that of your pitiful world! Consider my offer. Surrender the power, and I will call all the dead back to the underworld myself! I will save your pathetic world."

I hesitated. Could he really stop the apocalypse? Did the ends justify the means?

Gareth grabbed my shoulder, snapping me out of it. "Don't even think about it. He might end this apocalypse, but what he unleashes on the world could be far worse."

Dorian nodded in agreement, jaw set.

"Give me a minute to consider!" I called to Set, stalling for time. I turned to my companions and spoke low. "Any chance you guys could magic Aiden and Charlie to safety?"

Dorian and Sydney exchanged a look. "We'll give it our best shot," Gareth muttered.

"I think we can save them," Sydney added. "A prism. It should hold them over the water long enough for us to pull them out."

I cracked my knuckles, power rising within me. "Then it's ass-kicking time. I'll handle tall, red, and ugly."

Letting out a shriek as my makeshift war cry, I charged Set as he released his hostages. Gareth and Sydney were quick, though. They cast a pair of magical bubbles around Aiden and Charlie before the river could swallow them. Then, they hurried along the riverbank as the rapid current pulled them to who knew where. Even with my ancient memories, I wasn't entirely sure where the river led.

I turned back to Set as he roared in anger, massive fists

swinging. I ducked and weaved, using my smaller size to my advantage.

"You pathetic worm!" Set bellowed. "I offer you salvation, and you spit in my face!"

"Salvation, my ass!" I snapped back. "You want the power for yourself, you overgrown garden gnome!"

That must have hit a nerve because Set loosed an inhuman howl and came at me harder. I managed to land a few good hits with blasts of Isis' magic, but damn, he was fast for a big guy.

Even as I suspected I might be in over my head, Dorian was suddenly at my side. He grabbed my hand, golden eyes blazing like the sun. "We're stronger together," he told me. And I believed him.

As one, we unleashed a massive surge of power that sent Set flying into the sulfurous banks of the River Styx. The Lord of Chaos peeled himself from the muck, murder in his eyes.

"This isn't over!" he raged. "The deal is off! I will destroy your precious world and feast on your souls!"

"Bring it on, bitch," I taunted, readying myself for round two. This was gonna be one hell of a fight.

I glanced at Dorian, his hand still clasped firmly in mine. Our powers thrummed in unison, two hearts beating as one.

"You ready for this?" I asked.

He grinned, eyes glinting with anticipation. "I was born ready."

Together, we turned back to face Set, who was advancing with a murderous look on his grotesque face.

"Your arrogance will be your downfall, Isis!" the Lord of Chaos snarled. "I have existed since the dawn of time. Before the world, there was only chaos. You are but an ant beneath my foot!"

"Yeah, yeah, put a sock in it already," I shot back. Man, this guy loved the sound of his own voice. Time to take him down a peg or two.

I squeezed Dorian's hand, signaling him. We thrust our

entwined hands forward and unleashed a concentrated beam of pure light magic. It slammed into Set's chest, searing his flesh. He released an unearthly shriek as wisps of smoke curled from the wound.

Yet he remained standing, hate-filled eyes fixed on us.

"You'll have to do better than that," he rumbled.

Crap. Looked like I'd have to pull out the big guns. I closed my eyes, drawing deep on the well of power within. Light swelled through every molecule of my being as I tapped into the magic Ra had gifted me.

When I opened my eyes, they shone with divine radiance. I raised my free hand, weaving an intricate pattern in the air. The shape had simply flashed into my mind. I didn't even realize I knew it. A portal took shape, shimmering with unearthly light.

"Your reign of terror ends now, Set!" My voice echoed with ancient authority. "Go to jail, bitch! Go directly to jail!"

Dorian thrust his free fist forward, and the portal I'd made flew at Set like a fastball.

It enveloped Set, dragging the thrashing god into its luminous depths. With a final shriek, the Lord of Chaos vanished from sight.

The portal collapsed on itself, forming a sphere of light that floated back to my upturned palm. A pocket dimension. A prison for chaos and, if all went according to plan, the resurrected dead.

I clutched the glowing orb tight, still reeling from what we'd accomplished. We'd done it. We'd trapped Set, the jerkface god who'd been making life miserable. Now we could finally end this freaking zombie apocalypse and get back to our quasi-normal lives.

A caw pierced the air, and I glanced up to see a raven circling overhead. With a startled yelp, I leaped back as the bird dive-bombed me. At the last second, it shape-shifted into a tall, pale woman with wild dark hair. The Morrigan.

She stalked toward me, hand outstretched. "Give it to me! We had a deal, Isis."

I shook my head. "Uh, no, we didn't. The deal was you'd help heal the void. Didn't do that yet, and I don't need you now, so…"

The Morrigan's face contorted in fury. She raised her arms, summoning crackling dark energy between her palms.

Crap on a cracker. Looked like I'd have to fight this crazy goddess now, too.

Before she could strike, a flash of light blinded me momentarily.

When I could see again, Gareth, Sydney, Aiden, and Charlie appeared. My brother and boss were still suspended in floating magic bubbles.

"Guys, get back!" I yelled. "The Morrigan's lost her freaking mind!"

With a savage cry, the Morrigan attacked. A swirling vortex of inky darkness erupted from her hands, threatening to swallow us whole.

Gareth was faster. He traced a quick portal in the air and shouted, "Everybody in!"

We leaped through as the Morrigan's attack crashed down where we'd been standing. A split second later, we tumbled out the other side onto solid ground in the Underworld.

I picked myself up and dusted off my jeans. "Well, that was a thing."

"The Morrigan will be a problem," Dorian remarked. "We'll deal with her later. We need to get back and stop this damn apocalypse."

I nodded, looking at the glowing orb in my palm. My makeshift prison for the chaos god Set. Hard to believe we'd actually pulled it off.

"Let's get Aiden and Charlie down first," I suggested.

Gareth dismissed the magic bubbles, gently lowering my brother and boss to the ground. Charlie wobbled on his heels.

"Oh my God, I need a drink," he muttered.

Aiden shook his head, dazed. "Did we win?"

I grinned. "For now, but we've got bigger fish to fry." I waved the Set orb. "This bad boy should let me undo all the zombie mojo and save the world. So, y'know, no pressure."

"You can do it." Dorian squeezed my shoulder. "I believe in you, Briar."

His faith meant everything. With my friends at my side, I felt ready to take on anything.

"Let's go home," I announced.

Gareth opened one last portal. Earth lay beyond.

I clutched the orb tightly. A warm breeze hit my face. In the distance, the sun shone down on the Lake of the Ozarks.

Home. Time to clean up this mess and get my life back.

I turned to my friends. "Ready for this?"

Aiden cracked his knuckles. "Oh, I was born ready. Let's end this nightmare."

With my family beside me, I raised the orb high. "It's time to save the world."

The final battle awaited. Together, we would prevail.

CHAPTER TWENTY-NINE

Charlie's hands trembled as we stood by the shimmering portal back to Earth. His eyes were distant, staring into the mystical doorway leading home. A horde of the undead awaited us. I could only hope Gareth's shield had held. The fact that the portal still stood, and none had come through trying to reach Set, was a good sign.

"I don't know if I can do this," Charlie muttered. "Don't know if I'll come back the same." His fingers brushed the bare spot on his wrist where his pewter band used to be. "Don't even know if my soul's still intact."

I cupped his scruffy cheek. "Oh, Charlie." I slid off the band he'd given me what seemed like ages ago and clasped it back around his wrist. "You walked through hell and back, and you're still you. Your soul's tougher than old boots." I offered a faint smile. "If that Morrigan thinks she can take you, she's got another thing coming. We need our druid."

Charlie nodded, blinking hard. "If I turn murderous…"

I shrugged. "Then I'll come back with a boat and fish your soul out of that damn river. I'm not losing you, Charlie."

Charlie nodded again, more firmly this time. "All right, then. Let's do this."

The team gathered close. Dorian, Gareth, Sydney, Aiden. We stepped through the shimmering portal as one to emerge in the dim warehouse.

As I'd hoped, the giant glowing shield still stood, magical geometric patterns swirling across its surface. Beyond it, crowding the warehouse and gathered outside, was a writhing sea of the undead. Their enraged eyes and gaping mouths pressed against the shield, desperate to reach us. To reach Set.

I raised my hand and made a sharp, twisting motion. The portal to the underworld behind us collapsed with a faint *pop*.

Then I held out my palm. A glowing orb materialized above it. The prison dimension. This was the moment of truth.

I drew a deep breath and hurled the orb at the warehouse floor.

The portal swirled open, revealing only white emptiness within.

Gareth eyed it warily. "Are you certain Set cannot escape this realm?"

I nodded. "It has an entrance but no clear exit. The only way out is to endure a trial similar to what Ra put Dorian and me through. It takes great virtue and wisdom to pass."

"Impressive," Dorian remarked. "You made all that with a flick of the wrist?"

I grinned. "Pretty much. This power is something else. Never thought I'd be able to handle it."

"Brilliant move, Briar." Gareth looked at me with wide eyes. He loved me still, but he knew my heart was Dorian's. "Set will be stuck for quite some time. That pompous bastard wouldn't know virtue if it bit him in the ass."

We fanned out, ready to act. I turned to Gareth. "After you drop the shield, teleport Aiden and Charlie to safety."

"Of course."

Gareth dissolved the magical barrier with a wave of his hand. The creatures surged forward, their decaying hands grasping.

Instead of attacking, they hurled themselves into the glowing portal, one after another disappearing into the white void. It was working.

I nodded to Gareth. He clasped Aiden's and Charlie's shoulders and vanished, hopefully taking them somewhere secure. Probably back to the trailer or Charlie's bar.

Now, it was only Dorian, Sydney, and I left to witness the dead emptying into the prison like a river pouring into a lake. The more the dead disappeared, the more my anxiety waned. We'd done it. It was working.

I released a relieved sigh, but it hitched in my throat when a dark figure materialized before us.

Anubis. His jackal eyes blazed as he stared me down.

"Isis!" his voice boomed. "What have you done?"

I stood tall, pushing down my unease. "Stopped your little apocalypse. Delayed it, at least. Sorry, buddy, you'll have to save it for another time."

He prowled toward me, muscles taut. I thought he might attack. Shockingly, Anubis dropped to one knee before me.

"My queen," he rasped, head bowed in deference. "It shall be as you command."

I blinked, steadying my nerves. "Damn straight it will."

With that, the god of the dead vanished. I turned to Dorian and Sydney. "Well, that was new."

We watched the remaining resurrected continue their march into the void. My gambit had paid off. The apocalypse was averted for now. It hadn't been easy, but dealing with pissy gods was a small price to pay for protecting the mortal realm.

This would take a while. We'd have to keep an eye on the portal to make sure Set didn't somehow figure his way out. Still, this whole crazy gamble had actually worked. The realm glowed ominously as thousands of souls drained into its depths.

I nodded to Dorian. "Let's seal this thing up before any more surprises show. We'll have to survey the damage. If any dead folk are still wandering around, we can always open it again."

I waved a hand, and the portal shrank into a small ball that settled into my palm.

I sagged against Dorian, the adrenaline crash hitting me hard. He wrapped an arm around me and pressed a kiss into my hair.

"We did it," I murmured.

Sydney whooped, punching the air. "We told Death himself to shove it! Drinks are on me tonight."

I managed a tired smile. We'd beaten the odds and saved the world. Not bad for a hedge witch and her Ozark friends.

"Drinks will have to wait," I cautioned. "We still have to seal the veil. Anyone else who dies will go to the underworld with Anubis, but they can still cross the River Styx and reenter our world. I'd rather not be playing clean-up forever."

Sydney nodded. "I'll gather the ingredients."

"We'll need the stone circle," I added. "How much time do you need?"

"Give me an hour. I have most of it back at Morai HQ."

CHAPTER THIRTY

The cold concrete chilled my skin as I slid down the warehouse wall. Dorian's warmth beside me was the only relief from the damp air. We were waiting for Sydney to return with the goods.

"This curse is killing me, Briar," Dorian muttered, his breath ragged. "Even fighting alongside you all was pure agony."

I turned to look at him, taking in the dark circles under his eyes.

"I'm not sure how much more I can take," he whispered. His voice broke, and he dropped his head in his hands.

My heart shattered seeing him like this. I had to dig deep to find some glimmer of hope.

"We'll get through this," I told him, grasping his hand. "After the veil is healed, we'll figure the rest out. I promise."

Dorian lifted his head, meeting my gaze. The ghost of a smile crossed his lips. He squeezed my hand back gently. We sat in silence again, drawing strength from each other.

"First, we heal the veil, then we get out of here," I stated suddenly. "Out of this town. You and me."

Dorian turned to look at me, surprise in his eyes.

"We could start over somewhere new. Leave all this behind."

Dorian sighed, a sad smile on his face. "That's not fair to you, Briar. You have a life here."

I shook my head adamantly. "My life is with you now. I don't care where we go as long as we're together."

Dorian opened his mouth to respond when a brilliant glow filled the warehouse. I shielded my eyes against the blinding light.

A familiar voice boomed. "Well said, Isis."

The light receded, and I blinked to see Ra standing before us.

"What are you doing here?" I asked warily. Dorian tensed beside me.

"There is an unfinished matter we must attend to." Ra's gaze burned into mine.

I glanced at Dorian nervously. "What do you mean?"

"The two of you must be joined in sacred matrimony," Ra declared. "You cannot heal the veil otherwise. It will have the added benefit of breaking Dorian's curse."

My mouth fell open in shock. I looked at Dorian, heart hammering. Was I ready for this?

Dorian met my wide-eyed stare and gave a slight nod. He was ready. And with him by my side, so was I.

I inhaled deeply and turned back to Ra. "All right. I'm ready."

Dorian moved to stand beside me. "As am I."

Ra's stern face softened into a smile. "Excellent. Join hands, my children."

I laced my fingers through Dorian's, pulse racing. His hand was warm and solid. Comforting.

Ra lifted his staff. "With the power vested in me by, well, me, I declare this couple bonded in holy matrimony. Through this union, may your curses be broken and your destinies aligned."

He brought the staff down with a *thud* that seemed to reverberate through my bones. "I now pronounce you husband and wife."

I turned to Dorian, heart swelling. His eyes locked with mine, more vulnerable than I'd ever seen them. He cupped my face gently and pressed his lips to mine.

Warmth flooded through me at the contact. For a blissful moment, nothing else existed but Dorian's kiss.

When we finally broke apart, Ra lifted his hands. "May the gods bless this union. Use your bond wisely to heal the veil between worlds and to protect the Earth forevermore."

I tilted my head, still giddy from the kiss. "So, this marriage will give us the power to heal the veil together?"

Ra nodded. "It will indeed. The consummation of your bond will unleash magic potent enough to mend the tear."

I laughed. "Consummation, huh? Not sure you know what that means, old man."

Ra chuckled, a deep rumbling sound. "I'm well aware of the modern implications, my dear. In this case, I speak of the metaphysical consummation. The full realization of your mystical union."

"Ah, gotcha." I winked at Dorian. "Plenty of time for the other kind later."

Before Ra could respond, a commotion at the warehouse entrance drew our attention. Sydney hurried in, her arms full of cloth bags and vials.

"I've got the goods!" she called. Behind her followed Gareth, Aiden, Charlie, and over a dozen women in dark robes. Witches from the Morai coven.

I blinked in surprise as Sydney dumped the ingredients at my feet. "I thought we could use some extra magical oomph, so I brought help." She jerked her thumb at the assembled witches.

"Yeah, there's no way we're lettin' you fix this veil thing alone," Gareth added, stepping forward.

Aiden bobbed his head eagerly. "We're here for ya, sis."

I looked between their determined faces, heart swelling. "You guys…thank you."

Ra folded his arms, nodding in approval. "Well, then. Shall we proceed?"

I turned to Dorian and squeezed his hand, ready to embrace our destiny together. "Let's do this."

Sydney began passing out bundles of herbs, crystals, and vials of viscous liquid to the Morai witches. "Okay, ladies, let's make some magic!"

The witches formed a circle on the warehouse floor. At Sydney's direction, they simultaneously crushed the herbs and crystals in their fists, chanting in an ancient tongue. Wisps of colored smoke rose from their hands, filling the air with sweet aromas.

I felt the power building as the witches released the essences into the circle. The carved runes glowed, etching the floor in shimmering light.

"Now, channel your energy into the circle!" I commanded.

The witches thrust their hands downward. Streams of pure magical force flowed from their fingertips. Runes appeared on the floor, geometric patterns with intersecting lines. The entire place thrummed with mystical energy.

Dorian and I stepped into the center of the circle with our hands still clasped. Our feet aligned with the central rune, etched with the symbol of infinity.

While looking into Dorian's eyes, I drew on my ancient magic. Not only what Ra gave me, or even what came from my past life, but my own.

Together, we focused the swirling magic into a shimmering veil only we could see. I visualized the torn, golden fabric and willed our combined power to knit it back together. The tear slowly mended before my mind's eye, the veil becoming whole once more.

The air crackled a final time as the last of the magic faded away. I exhaled, leaning into Dorian.

"It's done," I announced. "The veil is mended."

Dorian smiled, brushing a strand of hair from my face. "We did it, love."

I nodded, suddenly feeling the weight of exhaustion from expending so much mystical energy. Using ancient magic always took its toll.

A harsh caw echoed through the warehouse, making us all jump. A raven burst from a broken window, its inky wings spread wide.

My heart dropped into my stomach. "The Morrigan."

"The Phantom Queen?" Sydney gasped.

I watched the raven disappear into the night sky. "She knows the veil is repaired. She won't wait long to make her next move."

Dorian's arm wrapped around me. "Then we'll be ready for her."

The others nodded, determination in their eyes.

Ra stepped forward, the light of the full moon reflecting on his pale skin. "You all have done a great thing here tonight. I have faith that you will be able to stand against whatever this foreign goddess has planned." He looked at me and Dorian in turn before continuing.

"My time on this plane is up, but my spirit will always be with you," he stated before he faded away.

I watched as he disappeared, tears streaming down my face. I barely knew him—as Briar, anyway. As Isis, he and I had a long and complicated history. Still, what mattered most wasn't the past. It was the present and the future. Ra had given us so much. A mission, a purpose, and most of all, hope for the future. None of that would have happened without my friends. Without my witches. Hedges, Morai, and druid alike.

CHAPTER THIRTY-ONE

The clang of a bell snapped me to attention. "Order up, Briar!" Aiden called as he slapped two more patties on the grill. The sizzle and smell of burgers on the flattop always got my stomach growling.

I hustled over and grabbed the overflowing plates. A double bacon cheeseburger with extra fries for the couple in the back booth and a chicken salad sandwich with a pickle spear the old-timer in the John Deere cap wanted.

I delivered the food and topped off some iced teas on my way back to the bar. Charlie was leaning across the worn wood as Grace chatted him up about who knows what. Those two could babble all day if you let 'em.

In the corner booth, Dorian, Gareth, and Sydney passed a pitcher of Bud Light between them. I still couldn't quite wrap my mind around that trio. They used to be enemies, my new hubby and Gareth. Sydney was a go-between for a while, but she was Morai at the end of the day. However, we'd all been through hell and back lately. I guessed near-death experiences had a way of bringing people together.

"How's it going over here?" I asked, dropping more napkins on their table. "Need a refill?"

"I think we're set for now." Gareth's Ken-doll face looked relaxed for once. "Thank you, Briar."

I gave them a dimpled smile before moving on.

I was heading back behind the bar when the front door swung open, and in marched Deputy Jones with a few other uniforms behind him. The chatter in the place quieted a notch as all eyes turned their way. Par for the course whenever cops showed up.

Jonesy went directly to Charlie, and they talked across the bar. I hovered nearby, wiping down the bar top, keeping an ear turned in their direction. After a minute, Charlie looked over and called, "Briar, can you step into my office for a minute?"

I nodded, my stomach tightening. Jonesy gave me a polite tip of his hat as I came around the bar. Charlie led the way, and we filed into his small, cluttered office behind the kitchen.

"What's this about?" I asked, leaning against the wall opposite Charlie's desk.

Jonesy removed his hat and met my eyes. "I wanted to come by and apologize formally. I know you and your friends had something to do with resolving our...problem. The sheriff and I agreed to keep it quiet officially, but I wanted you to know I appreciate whatever you did."

I studied his face, looking for any hint of insincerity, but he seemed earnest. "I'm just glad it's over," I finally told him.

Jonesy nodded. "Well, if anything else strange comes up, I hope you'll consider assisting us again."

I blinked in surprise. "Well, that's a change in policy. You want me to *help* the police?"

Jonesy nodded. "The sheriff's department. The local police aren't entirely in the loop."

I shrugged. "Police. Sheriffs. Six of one, you know."

Jonesy cleared his throat. "Not really, but that doesn't matter. The point is, it seems you have a knack for handling the weird cases. Honestly, we've been in over our heads. This is more than we can deal with alone, and I get the sense more of those are coming our way."

I chewed my lip. Teaming up with the cops was not something I'd ever envisioned for myself.

"I appreciate the offer," I remarked slowly. "I'd be happy to lend a hand when I can."

Jonesy broke into a grin and pulled something from his pocket. "Glad to hear it." He handed me a shiny silver badge.

I turned it over in my palm. "Deputy Witch, huh?" I couldn't help but chuckle. "I like the sound of that."

Jonesy tipped his hat again. "You let me know if you need anything. We'll be in touch."

After he left, Charlie looked at me and laughed. "Well, ain't that something. Who'd have thought?"

I sighed, tucking the badge into my apron pocket. "With the Morrigan still out there planning the gods know what, I suspect I'll have my hands full soon enough."

Charlie pulled me into a quick hug. "You know I'm always here for you. Whatever you need."

I gave him a grateful smile before pulling away. "Right now, I need to get back to my customers. I think table six is waiting on their burgers."

Charlie waved me off. "Go on then, Deputy. Right now, you're still Deputy Waitress. Serve tables and protect."

I rolled my eyes but couldn't help grinning as I headed back to the bar.

I weaved through the crowded tables, my head still spinning from the unexpected turn of events. Who would've thought my chaotic life would lead me down such an official path?

I glanced at Dorian, Gareth, and Sydney, still chatting and laughing in their corner booth. Part of me wished I could join them, share a pitcher of beer, and decompress. Yet duty called in more ways than one now.

Table nine flagged me down, ready to order another round. I plastered a cheerful smile on my face and got back to work, pushing thoughts of the Morrigan and my new "job" to the back of my mind.

"What can I get for y'all?" I asked, pulling out my order pad.

The middle-aged couple rattled off their requests, which I jotted down quickly. As I turned to put in their order, I felt a chill run down my spine. Outside, on one of the porch rails overlooking the lake, was a raven.

The Morrigan was watching. Biding her time.

I headed out the door, but as I approached, she spread her wings and flew away.

As I stood there, watching her disappear into the distance, a strange feeling washed over me. It was as if I could feel her presence lingering in the air. I shook my head, trying to clear my mind, but the feeling persisted.

Suddenly, a hand fell on my shoulder. I spun to see Dorian standing behind me with concern etched on his face.

"Briar, are you okay?" he asked, his voice laced with worry.

I shook my head. "It's that damned Morrigan. She's watching us. She still thinks I owe her, but you know, she didn't do what we agreed."

"She did help us, though. Back in the underworld."

"Yeah, but that wasn't the deal."

Dorian nodded and placed a hand on my back. "We've handled worse, you know. You kicked Set's ass. We thwarted a zombie apocalypse. How much worse could it be?"

I drew a deep breath. "You're right. Whatever she's up to, whenever she plays her hand, I'll be ready."

AUTHOR NOTES - THEOPHILUS MONROE

I know you're worried about me. After I told you I'd stepped on a nail (see the author notes at the end of *Lady of the Lake*) I was a little hobbled for a while. But now I'm good…

It is well, it is well… with my sole.

Ok, I've been holding on to that one for a while. Dad jokes are afoot! (sorry). I can feel the groans already vibrating back at me through my keyboard.

Now that I've assuaged your worries about my minor injury, I'm going to write a little about how it's important to take a "pause" every now and again. A little time to reflect, recharge, and enjoy life.

I've decided to take a short "break" on writing. Just through the holidays.

Over the last four years, I've written *a lot* of books. I have a few in the queue, ready to go, so most readers won't notice a huge decline in the frequency of my releases, but this is the last book I had ready for this series.

I have enough books out there that I can afford a break. What's life worth if we're always "working" to get where we want to go but never stop to appreciate how far we've come?

There's always a chance that life will pass us by while we spend our entire lives trying to build for a future that we'll never enjoy—because even then, we'll be caught up in the addiction to "progress," to achieving "more" that we fail to appreciate what we've worked for.

I have three young boys at home. So, this holiday season, I'm spending my time with them. Less time behind a keyboard. It won't be long before the "magic" of the holidays is lost on my kids, and I don't want to miss it.

Chances are, I'll write a bit on break. I'm a writer. I can't just turn that part of me off. But I'll probably write less for production and more for the pure enjoyment of it. I'll write when the muse strikes, not when my schedule tells me it's time.

But I will be back, recharged, and ready to fill your e-reader in the new year.

The question I have for you is this: Do you want more Briar Bloom?

The first two books sold better than I expected. The series is a little different from my other series. There's more romance at the center of the story, and the setting isn't urban. But if there's a part of this series I've enjoyed the most, it's the Ozarks milieu. It's one of my favorite places to be, so it makes sense I'd have fun writing a story there.

So, if you want more from the *Hedge Witch Diaries,* let us know! You can do so in a review, by dropping a note on our Facebook pages, or by shooting an e-mail my way.

-Theo

AUTHOR NOTES - MICHAEL ANDERLE

DECEMBER 6, 2023

First off, thank you from the depths of my overactive mind for joining Theophilus and myself in yet another written adventure. And a special shoutout to those of you who've stuck around for these author notes—it's like the secret track at the end of an old CD, and you're the cool kids who found it.

Walking in Theophilus's Shoes... and Why I Can't Sit Still

So, here's a confession: Much like Theophilus from his latest escapade, I'm relentlessly driven to forge ahead. The act of stopping to smell the proverbial roses? I'm not great at it.

There's this annoying feeling that if I pause for even a moment, the ferocious beast of the future now will trample me underfoot. Publishing waits for no one, and in this digital age, neither does writing.

But here's the rub—I can sense the toll it's taking.

Both body and soul are waving little white flags, signaling a need for respite. I'm in Cabo San Lucas as I write this, a place where time seems to saunter, and the biggest decision of the day is whether to have fish or shrimp tacos. Theoretically, it's the perfect spot to recharge. Go out, walk amongst the sand and sea ... Get healthy, you know?

And yet, the mere thought of 'exercise for the sake of health' has me lumping it into the work category. I mean, if we're being honest, walking feels a lot like effort, and I've convinced myself I'm on a break from that particular four-letter word, right?

But the mind is a tricky creature, and mine is currently bending into pretzel shapes, attempting to justify dodging what's good for me. Am I a master of mental gymnastics, skirting around activities I'd rather avoid? It's likely.

A Tangent, A Wife, and A Moment of Clarity

In the midst of this internal debate, I'm reminded that I'm about to pick up my wife from the airport. That's something I'm genuinely looking forward to—there's no work involved, just the pure joy of being in the presence of someone I've missed dearly. That's my good deed for the day, and it feels like a holiday in itself.

So, maybe there's a lesson in there for me (and perhaps for you, too). Maybe it's not about finding grand moments of leisure but embracing the small joys, the simple pleasures that life tosses our way. Maybe it's about recognizing that, while the relentless march of progress won't slow down, our appreciation of life's intermissions can give us the strength to keep up without burning out.

Weaving Tales and Taking Notes

I hope you've enjoyed the latest story and that, in between the lines, you've found a bit of yourself. I'm curious to hear how you take a breather from the hustle. What's your secret to savoring life amidst the chaos? Feel free to share in the book review comments—if you're so inclined.

Now, if you'll excuse me, I'm off to collect my better half and make the most of our time together. And who knows? I might even take that dreaded walk... eventually.

Until our paths cross again in the pages to come,

Ad Aeternitatem,

Michael Anderle

PS: MORE STORIES with Michael newsletter HERE: https://
michael.beehiiv.com/

213

Michael Anderle

PS: MORE STORIES with Michael newsletter HERE: https://
michael.beehiiv.com/

Scared Shiftless

Bat Shift Crazy

No Shift, Sherlock

Shift for Brains

Shift Happens

Shift on a Shingle

The Vilokan Asylum of the Magically and Mentally Deranged

The Curse of Cain

The Mark of Cain

Cain and the Cauldron

Cain's Cobras

Crazy Cain

The Wrath of Cain

The Blood Witch Saga

Voodoo and Vampires

Witches and Wolves

Devils and Dragons

Ghouls and Grimoires

More to come!

FREE URBAN FANTASY ADVENTURE: DRUIDESS (GET IT HERE!)

GoE OMNIBUS COLLECTIONS [in Chronological Order]:

The Druid Legacy

Wyrmrider (Books 1-4)

The Voodoo Legacy

The Legacy of a Vampire Witch

The Legend of Nyx

The Vilokan Asylum of the Magically and Mentally Deranged

Other Theophilus Monroe Series

CONNECT WITH THE AUTHORS

Connect with Theophilus Monroe

Website: www.theophilusmonroe.com

Social Media
https://www.facebook.com/pages/category/Author/
Theophilus-Monroe-Urban-Fantasy-Author-101469961530864/

Connect with Michael Anderle

Website: http://lmbpn.com

Email List: https://michael.beehiiv.com/

https://www.facebook.com/LMBPNPublishing

https://twitter.com/MichaelAnderle

https://www.instagram.com/lmbpn_publishing/

https://www.bookbub.com/authors/michael-anderle